Dead Man's Handle

JOHN
BLACKBURN

Dead Man's Handle

JONATHAN CAPE
THIRTY BEDFORD SQUARE LONDON

First published 1978
© 1978 by John Blackburn

Jonathan Cape Ltd, 30 Bedford Square, London WC1

British Library Cataloguing in Publication Data

Blackburn, John
Dead man's handle.
I. Title
823'.9'IF   PR6052.L34D/
ISBN 0-224-01417-X

Printed in Great Britain by The Anchor Press Ltd
and bound by Wm Brendon & Son Ltd
both of Tiptree, Essex

To Peter Betton

... And all unseen
Romance brought up the nine-fifteen.
KIPLING

Preface

On November 1st, at 21.15 precisely, a signal turned to green, the Channel Belle from London to Lythborne slid out of Trafalgar Road Terminus; the terror began. Twelve coaches behind the Warrior class diesel-electric locomotive, *Marshal Ney*; 636 passengers, one ticket collector and four buffet-car attendants on board; gross load, 418 tons. Guard – Charles Mills; driver – William Smith; co-driver – Richard Andrews.

'Dead on time as usual, Billy. They always keep a clear line for the old 9.15.' Dick Andrews was an elderly man almost due to retire and, like most of his kind, he shunned foreign terminology. As far as he was concerned, the evening Channel Belle was the *9.15* and always would be. 'You must be feeling pretty proud of yourself, lad. Your first trip in charge of her, ain't it?' He glanced at his companion with a touch of envy as the heavy locomotive crossed a set of points and rumbled over the Thames bridge. He'd been forty-three before they entrusted him with a main-line express and Smith was only in his early twenties. Too young for such responsibility in Andrews's opinion, but the boy seemed a good, steady type and he had tradition to help him, because the railway was in his blood. His father and his grandfather and his great-grandfather had all been drivers and Andrews had known the father well. Poor, boastful Peter Smith, who'd called himself the King of the Road till that damned night on the Crematorium Bend. Not his fault, whatever the scandal-mongers said. Andrews hadn't liked his colleague, but though the man boasted, he was as strong as an ox and he didn't drink on duty. Peter Smith never would have blacked out and lost control of a train.

'Aye, your first run of the Belle, lad, and probably my last. At the end of the week I'll be retired and slung on the scrap heap. Dunno whether I'm looking forward to it or not.' Andrews considered the prospect. It would be pleasant to lie in bed as long as he liked, to potter in the garden and sit watching the telly; to be a senior citizen, a gentleman of leisure. He'd earned his retirement, but it might also be bloody boring and he thought nostalgically of the past. Forty-seven years on the railways and there were a lot of things to remember. The Blitz, for example, and the morning when a German fighter had come screaming down at them while Harry Godwin hurried the Pullman towards the safety of Greystone Tunnel. The day when he was firing for Mike Scott and they'd done a ton down Chalford bank. How the shed-master had cursed when he heard the old steamer come clanking home with a fractured bearing. How he and Harry had celebrated their triumph in the local.

The good times and the bad times, the times which were nearly over. He was a has-been already, acting as assistant to a boy, and soon he'd be a back number, though he was lucky, or luckier than some. He had his health and strength, which was more than you could say of others. Andrews glanced at Billy Smith again. A nice-looking lad, rather like his father had looked before the train ran away and he copped it. Like his father physically, but not mentally. Peter Smith called himself the King of the Road because he was a flogger and this boy was dawdling. Dick Andrews frowned at the speedometer and the throttle lever. Only fifty miles an hour and scarcely half-power. Peter Smith would have clocked up sixty-five by now and the engine would be starting to sing.

'Come on, Bill,' he said. 'We've got a fine clear night and there's a clear road ahead of us. No restrictions till the Crem Bend, so give her the gun, boy, and show the passengers what you can do. They've paid for their journey, so let 'em have a run for their money. Get 'em to Lythborne before time.

'Why, what's the matter?' In the reflection of the panel lights he saw that the young man's forehead was beaded with sweat and his eyes were haunted. 'Not nervy are you ... not superstitious?' Though Andrews knew why the driver was anxious he spoke mockingly. Billy Smith had a reason for anxiety, but no excuse for it. Nerves and locomotives did not mix and the dead were best forgotten. The boy had to forget his father and pull himself together, to prove himself and show what he could do. 'If you're too scared to drive I'd best take over.'

'I'm not scared, but I feel a bit strange, Mr Andrews.' The haunted eyes flicked from the dials to the signals ahead and then to a sky sign on a high building flashing out the date and the time, advertisements and news items.

'NOVEMBER 1st ... 2100 hours, 22 minutes ... BEER DRINKERS DRINK BUXTON'S BITTER ... 2100 hours, 23 minutes ... DOCK STRIKE CONTINUES.' The minutes and the announcements might change, but the date remained constant and it never would change; not for him, not for William Smith. November 1st ... Dad's Day ... Simon's Day ... The Day of Disaster ... The Night of the Crippled King.

'Can you blame me for being a bit edgy, Mr Andrews? Don't you know what happened on the Crem Bend ... Dad's accident?'

'Your father never had an accident, Billy. His train was derailed because a couple of murderous kids concussed him, and if I'd got my hands on the bastards they'd have paid for what they did.' Andrews flexed his muscles at the

9

thought. He might be old and backnumbered, but he was still strong and active. Quite strong enough to kill a couple of children. 'In any case the Crem derailment was three years ago and the murderers won't strike a second time, so forget 'em, son. Forget 'em and let her go. Get on ... get your hand over ... get crackin'.

'Ah, that's more like it.' Richard Andrews was rather pleased by his emphatic repetition of *get*, but he was much more pleased by the reaction which followed. Billy Smith had swung the throttle hard over, the train surged forward and he heard the sounds he loved. The pounding diesels and the whirr of the electric motors; singing wheels, clicking points and the roar of stations shooting past. *Marshal Ney* was a stupid name for a British locomotive, but she was a racehorse and Billy Smith had started to drive her like one. The speedometer needle was rising and the Channel Belle was rushing down to Lythborne. Out through the London suburbs; out into the country and on to the sea; on towards the Cemetery Bridge and the Crem Bend; on to the end of her journey.

Sixty-five ... Seventy-five ... Eighty miles an hour; the signals at green, the track as smooth as glass and the needle still rising. He'd told young Billy to give the engine her head and the lad had lost his anxieties. Billy Smith would keep on accelerating till they reached the slack and Peter Smith should be proud of his son. The King was finished and the Prince ruled his kingdom.

Richard Andrews could also be proud for lulling the boy's fears and he leaned comfortably back in his seat and prepared to enjoy the ride. Billy's first down-trip in charge of the old Belle and probably his own last trip on her. Why shouldn't he enjoy himself and relax? The train was in safe hands, so why shouldn't he close his eyes and hum in tune to the sounds he loved: the wheels and the motors, the song of speed?

No reason, apart from regulations, but it was a pity that the song became so loud that he didn't hear his driver cry out as the Cemetery Bridge hurtled towards them. A pity that he didn't open his eyes in time to see the horror in the driver's eyes or what the driver was staring at. A pity that he was too relaxed to brace himself when the song changed to a howl of tortured metal and the cab shuddered and jolted and threw him forward.

Such a shame that old Dicky Andrews never completed his final journey.

One

'You've really gone and done it, haven't you, son? You panicked and delayed a train for one-and-a-half hours. You strained the locomotive's transmission. You created chaos on the entire section.' Lt.-Col. Archibald Hector Vayne, M.C., sat glowering at Billy Smith. 'You also broke a large amount of glass and crockery and upset, injured and annoyed a large number of people. Twelve passengers and a buffet-car attendant were treated for shock, cuts and bruises, your co-driver was concussed, and the complaints are still pouring in.' Vayne rasped the last statement with fury because many of the complaints had been directed against himself. He was a senior security supervisor of British Rail's South-Eastern Region and if Smith's story was true he'd have some explaining of his own to do.

Not that the story was true of course. Sheer funk had made the boy jam on the brakes and reverse the locomotive, and no one had intended to sabotage the Belle … no one at all. The Colonel relaxed slightly and took a cigar from his case, looking pointedly at Dr Margaret Puxton, the station medical officer, while he lit it. Maggie Puxton considered that smoking was a wanton, disgusting hazard to health and Pamela had often called it the selfish, senseless extravagance of a senseless, selfish, idle man. What did he care? He had money to burn and if your number's on the bullet you'll cop it anyway. Maggie was a sanctimonious scaremonger and to hell with her. The Colonel blew a puff of smoke towards his colleague and was pleased to see her wince.

To hell with Pamela too, though she was probably there already; nagging the other damned souls and accusing the Devil of breaking her heart. He'd suspected that Pam was an objectionable woman before their engagement, but it was unfair to say that he'd married her for money. He'd only *married where money was*, and Pam had left him comfortably provided for, as the lower orders phrased it.

Very comfortably provided for, thank you kindly. With Pam's capital and his army pension and his present salary he was a rich man and he could be as extravagant and self-indulgent as he bloody well liked. The Colonel pulled at the cigar again and a second cloud of smoke drifted around Mr Emrys Evans, the N.U.R. representative, another canting killjoy whom he'd loathed since their first meeting.

Extravagant—yes. Selfish—yes. Idle—no. Archibald Vayne enjoyed his job, which he'd only held for six months, and he didn't want to lose it. Six pleasant months, but they'd gained him a lot of influential enemies. The Chief Regional Administrative Officer, the Deputy Regional Traffic Superintendent, the Station Manager of Trafalgar Road Terminus. (Manager indeed! Why didn't they use the term Station Master any more?) Also Brother Emrys Evans and Ted Morcom, his own assistant, and Dr Margaret Puxton, M.D. (Cantab.). They all wanted to see his head roll into the guillotine basket, and they'd all be disappointed, because Archie Vayne had a hard head and a stiff neck on his shoulders. Archie Vayne wasn't going to look through the little window; others were. The fools who had forgotten William Smith's background and put him in charge of the evening Belle to Lythborne. The old 9.15 that had run away on the Crematorium Bend three years ago, crippling Smith's father and carrying Pamela off to fresh fields and pastures new.

'Yes, you've gone and done it, lad,' he repeated. 'You've

14

annoyed a large number of people and worst of all you've annoyed me.' Vayne liked bullying subordinates and he removed the cigar from his lips and brandished it like a pistol. 'During the last few weeks, I've persuaded the magistrates to deal out really stiff sentences for vandalism and hooliganism, and no one would have dared to sabotage your train.' He glanced at the typed report for the tenth time, and when he looked up his tone changed and became soft and persuasive. 'We won't blame you, my boy. Not if you're frank and tell us the truth. You imagined that you saw a man leaning over the bridge parapet with some kind of missile in his hands, didn't you? You were thinking about your father and you started to relive his experience in your mind. Imagination was responsible for your panic. That's what made you jam on the brakes and reverse the locomotive, so why not admit it? There was nobody leaning on the parapet and a sudden brainstorm forced you to stop the train so violently that crockery and glass were broken ... that people were thrown to the floor and luggage hurtled from the racks on top of them ... why your partner, Richard Andrews, is in hospital with a suspected skull fracture.'

'There was a man or a boy on the bridge, Colonel, and he would have thrown something at the cab if I hadn't stopped the train.' Though he was still shaken and four pairs of eyes were studying him, Billy Smith spoke calmly and with absolute assurance. 'Of course I was thinking of my father, and what's abnormal about that? Dad was crippled for life on the Crem Bend and his co-driver and twenty-eight passengers died because some bastard or bastards smashed his windscreen with a rock. Dad was only half-conscious after the rock hit the glass and he never realized that his hand was on the throttle. The court of enquiry agreed that Dad failed to observe the speed restriction because of his injuries and the derailment was caused by sabotage. The court didn't blame Dad, sir. He was the best driver on the line, but those swine had it in for him.'

'We are not talking about your father's accident, Smith, and the tribunal was quite right to exonerate him. I certainly never blamed your father, though I was involved in the derailment myself and suffered a most grievous and tragic loss.' Archibald Vayne sighed sadly, but he remembered his feelings at the time, all the time – before, during and after the accident – and no sadness was involved. He'd felt anger and hatred and fear, disgust and elation.

They had had a jolly little session at the club, he and Tubby Tibbs and old Major-General Ponser. Best of all, the vintage 4½-litre Invicta, which was his pride and joy, had recently been tuned and he was looking forward to driving her down to Solly Kahn's place near Lythborne. Like most rich Yids, Solly and Rachel were lavish hosts and their week-end guests got red-carpet treatment. A luxurious country house, filled with flunkeys, excellent food and a cellar which was even more excellent. A good time should have been had by all, but as usual Pamela spoiled it.

'You're drunk, Archibald. Vilely, repulsively and incapably drunk and I'm not putting my life in your hands.' Pam had marched into the men's bar, where she had no right to be, and she flushed with indignation when he staggered slightly while walking to greet her. No fault of his that the floor was too highly polished and her entry had startled him. He hadn't expected the bitch for another ten minutes.

'We will leave the Invicta here and go to Lythborne by train. The Kahns' chauffeur can meet us at the station.' Pam was a keen rider to hounds and her voice cracked like a huntsman's whip, first at him and then at an aged retainer who had followed her into the room. 'Telephone

Lady Rachel Kahn at this number and deliver this message, porter.' She had scribbled the orders on a beer mat. 'Have our car garaged ... book two first-class seats on the Channel Belle ... send for a taxi.

'And when the taxi gets here, porter ... ' The last crack of the whip had been the unkindest cut of all. 'You had better assist Colonel Vayne down the steps and see that he doesn't reel into the gutter.'

Poor, cruel, intolerant Pamela ... Poor, cowardly, untrusting Pamela. If Pam had trusted him to drive she might still be alive, though thank God she wasn't. Thank God that she'd taken a window seat and he was dozing off when the carriage started to sway and he'd hardly noticed the wheels leave the rails and lurch towards the embankment. Thank God that there was a fat woman sitting opposite him and her warm, soft body had cushioned his fall. Thank God that he hadn't heard Pam's spine crack as her cold, skinny body hit the shattered window frame.

Thank God for everything. Poor, dead, intolerant Pam ... Rich, free, lucky Archie. Though the derailment had frightened him, he suffered no physical injuries and one might almost say that the people responsible for the crash had done him a favour, though purely by chance. The saboteurs couldn't have known that he and Pam would be on the train and nobody would ever know about the letter Pam had written to her solicitor and forgotten to post.

A horrible, mean letter composed by a horrible, mean-minded woman and it was a bit of luck that he found the envelope before the maid. Mr Evans was questioning Billy Smith and Vayne considered his wife's intentions. Pam had decided to apply for a divorce on the grounds of mental cruelty and cut him out of her will. That hadn't really surprised him, but the last paragraphs made him gasp because he had never imagined the extent of human treachery. Pam suspected that he'd been dipping into the regimental mess fund and felt it her duty to call at the Ministry of Defence and advise the Auditor General to cast a sharp eye over the books. If that eye had been cast, there'd have been no pension and no pleasant job with British Rail. He'd have been courtmartialled, disgraced and imprisoned.

Yes, two pieces of luck, two fortunate coincidences had saved his bacon, but Vayne didn't like coincidences and he looked at a report of the accident that had saved him from Pam's venom. When the driver, young Smith's father, had been able to speak, he'd stated that just before his cab windscreen was shattered, he had distinctly seen two figures leaning over the parapet of the bridge. Peter Smith couldn't say whether the figures were male or female, or what age group they belonged to. He seemed to think that one was a boy and the other a girl, but he couldn't be sure and the tribunal hadn't criticized him for that. The express was travelling fast, he had only caught a brief glimpse of his attackers and, in these days of long hair and sloppy clothes, it was often difficult to distinguish a man from a woman except in the buff.

Not all men, of course. Some had masculinity stamped on them like a hallmark. There was a mirror at the end of the room and Vayne lowered the report form and eyed his reflection proudly. A smart, expertly tailored jacket shrouding a trim, muscular torso without an ounce of surplus flesh on it. A strong, handsome face with a white scar, which many women found attractive, running down the left cheek. A thick crop of neatly trimmed brown hair with only a hint of grey at the temples. Fifty-six next birthday, but he didn't look a day over forty-five. A fine, military figure with a pair of steely blue eyes showing frankness, courage and determination.

'Too frank … too courageous … too bloody honest,'

Pam had once said. 'Your face is a mask, Archie, and you've got the eyes of a con man.'

Pam was right in a sense. Vayne hadn't resented her accusations, because he rather prided himself on winning people's confidence. The ability to look an interviewer straight in the face, the firm, dry handshakes, even though the rest of his body might be sweating with emotion. The modest admissions and the assuring promises. 'I'm no genius, sir, but you can rely on me to do my best. I always have done and I always will; can't say more than that.'

'I've told you the truth, ladies and gentlemen, and I can't say any more than that.' The words might have been repetitions of his own and Vayne looked sharply at Billy Smith who had refused the offer of a seat and was standing in front of his questioners. 'I made a statement to Mr Morcom last night and I will not change a single word of it.' Though Smith had been interrogated for almost an hour now, his tone remained assured and his eyes were calm. Eyes which were also rather like his own, Vayne thought and if he was in the boy's position he'd have refused a seat and stood facing the group at the table. Strange that a twenty-two-year-old youth with a board school education and a cockney accent should remind him of himself. Of Colonel Archibald Hector Vayne, M.C., Harrow and Sandhurst and the Royal Corps of Engineers. What were the links between them? What had they in common? Vayne frowned as a possible answer crossed his mind. Was William Smith another con man?

'The fact that Dick Andrews didn't see anyone on the bridge doesn't prove a thing, Doctor. I'm not saying that Dick was unobservant, but he's an elderly chap and his sight may not be as good as mine.' The boy had replied to Maggie Puxton and Vayne's suspicions and respect increased. *May not be*, instead of *can't be*. Just the right touch of charitable humility; exactly what he'd have said if he were in Smith's shoes and he listened intently to the next answer.

'Of course I don't resent your questions, ladies and gentlemen, and under the circumstances you have good reason to think I might have panicked. The circumstances and the coincidences: same train, almost the same time, and on the same stretch of line.' At long last William Smith was showing tension and Vayne watched him finger his tie. 'The same date too, November 1st, the day of my Dad's crash and the coincidence did worry me.

'No, that's untrue. I was more than worried when the foreman said I'd been detailed to drive the 9.15. I was scared out of my wits and I crawled along till Dick Andrews told me to stop dawdling and put on speed. To forget about Dad and give the Belle her head.

'Scared, but not crazy, Colonel, and you must believe me.' He appealed to Vayne for support. 'There was a man or a boy on the Crem Bridge and he was holding something over the parapet. I dunno what the thing was, but I saw it clearly in the street lights and I knew he was going to drop it if I didn't stop the train. I saw what he intended as distinctly as I can see you now, sir. I could read his thoughts, and that's why I jammed on the brakes and reversed the engines.'

'You appear to be gifted with telepathy and abnormally keen vision, Billy. There was a police constable walking along the bridge at the time and he didn't notice any suspicious character loitering near the parapet.' Vayne spoke sceptically, but several possibilities were flicking through his brain. Smith had a persuasive tongue, but confidence tricksters were not the only people with the powers of persuasion. Maniacs could be persuasive. Paranoiacs and schizophrenics like George Heath and Neville Haigh, and the Boston Strangler. The mentally sick also possessed the powers to deceive themselves, and that must be the solution. The coincidences of time and place had produced a fit of temporary insanity and for a brief instance, Billy Smith had believed that he was his father. That if he didn't stop the train he would relive his father's agony.

Yes, that had to be it, because if Smith was telling the truth British Rail was in trouble. Some man, woman or child had attempted to reproduce a disaster which had happened three years ago. Someone who was obsessed by a particular date, a particular train and a particular stretch of line. Someone or some persons with a crazed hatred against the Belle, or a murderous grudge against the Smiths, father and son. Persons who had known that Billy Smith would be in charge of the 9.15. Persons who had succeeded once and failed once. Frustrated persons ... mad persons. Persons who would try again.

Archie Vayne hoped that no such persons existed. He hoped and prayed that Smith was a highly strung neurotic who would never be allowed to drive another locomotive. He wanted to break the boy and expose his neurosis. Most of all he wanted to drown his own fears and prove that the danger was over. To justify his job and state that the trains could run in safety.

'Eyesight, telepathy and a creative imagination, Smith. Please accept my congratulations.' Vayne's sneering rasp returned because the boy's candid manner had also returned and he knew he was acting. The eyes were too honest, too self-assured and he'd seen a similar assurance before, though he couldn't recall where or when or under what circumstances. A parade ground in India, a room in a German barracks, a target range near Aldershot? He just couldn't remember the time or the place or the man's name. He wasn't even sure what the man had raised to his mouth before he died. The end of a rifle barrel ... the muzzle of a revolver?

'Yes, you should be proud of your imagination, son, and maybe novel writing would have given your talents more scope than driving trains.' Vayne dismissed the past and looked at a page of the boy's personal dossier. 'William Henry Smith; born in Croydon on August 9th, 1956; height, five foot six inches; weight, 141 pounds. Father, Peter Smith; Mother, Dorothy Sylvia Smith, *née* Callington-Graves.'

Callington-Graves, a grandiose name for a railwayman's fiancée and it seemed to ring a bell, but once again Vayne's memory failed him and he read on. William Smith had been educated at Glendale Road Comprehensive School in South London and had gained five 'O' levels and two 'A' levels in Physics and Maths. He had joined the railway service on his eighteenth birthday and was considered a loyal, intelligent and dedicated employee; hence his early promotion to main-line driving. He lived at home with his parents and an elder sister, Elizabeth. He had been passed fit at his last medical examination and his hobbies were football and amateur dramatics. He had been offered a course of executive training and refused. A good report—maybe too good. Five 'O' levels and two 'A's! Why not a university or the executive college? Vayne wondered. Why a mere locomotive pusher? Was the boy too loyal and too dedicated? Was he also frustrated and bitter? Emrys Evans had outlined Smith's parental background: a history of engine driving which had been preserved for several generations, and that could explain a lot. Had family loyalty forced him to follow that tradition against his better judgment? Had the pride of the father unhinged the son? Maggie Puxton considered that the boy was mentally stable, but Vayne had no faith in her opinion, and he rapped the table and resumed his questioning.

'I am not lying, Colonel, and I am not insane.' Billy

Smith looked away from him and turned to the other members of the enquiry. To Margaret Puxton and Ted Morcom and Emrys Evans. 'There was a man on the bridge and I saw him before the train halted. I knew what he wanted to do then and I was right. I know I was right because after we stopped I saw his face and it wasn't like a human face. I felt that the Devil was grinning at me and laughing.

'You've gotter believe me, ladies and gentlemen. If I hadn't acted quickly Dick Andrews and I would have ended up like Dad and his mate and you'd have had a second crash on the curve.' He clenched his right hand as though clutching a throttle. 'Charlie Mills, the guard, couldn't have noticed that we was exceeding the speed restriction, and even if he had, the brakes wouldn't have checked us in time.' He paused and Vayne knew that his theory was right. William Smith had not only relived his father's crash, he was picturing one of his own. 'No, Charlie couldn't 'ave 'alted the engine. Three diesel units developing over 2000 horsepower, an 1100-volt generator, and six electric motors with twelve coaches behind 'em. Four hundred tons and the speed rising to ninety.'

'We all know the specifications and power of Warrior class locomotives, Billy, but I think we'd like to hear more about the Devil.' The Colonel felt sure that his case was proven and he stood up and chuckled. 'Did your fiendish figure have horns and wings and a forked tail? Did he fly away after he grinned at you, or did he vanish in a cloud of sulphur?' Vayne's mirth increased and he never heard the telephone ring or saw Ted Morcom answer it. 'Or maybe it wasn't the Devil who frightened you. Perhaps you spotted a vampire. Tell me about him, Billy ... describe your monster in detail. Who was playing Count Dracula yesterday evening: Christopher Lee, Boris Karloff, Bela Lugosi?'

'I'm not insane, sir, but let me think ... please let me try to remember.' Vayne was towering over him and Smith lowered his head. 'The sound of the motors was deafening when we got into the cutting, but old Dick Andrews was dozing away beside me. I saw the bridge clear in the lights ... I saw the speed restriction sign beyond it, and then ... then I saw that thing suddenly rear up over the parapet.' Billy Smith had cracked as Vayne hoped he would and his speech was slurred and barely audible. 'Thing – man – boy – devil? No, I'm not sure what I saw and the face is getting vague and shadowy now, though it was so clear at the time. A man or a boy wearing a devil mask, or maybe the ghost of a devil. The ghost of Simon Lent ... ' He nodded at the office floor. 'Yes, that's who was standing on the bridge, Colonel Vayne ... Poor Simple Simon, our dead brother.'

'A ghost, eh?' Vayne's point was proven and he patted Smith on the shoulder and beamed at Evans and Dr Puxton. 'I think we can adjourn this meeting now unless either of you are addicted to ghost stories. Hallowe'en and Christmas Eve with chestnuts roasting before the fire and candles glowing through turnip lanterns. Lovely, creepy yarns with the wind howling outside the door and the demons lurking behind the door; in this instance, a human door.' He tapped his forehead with a recently manicured finger-nail and beamed again at his acumen and wit. 'Romance is a fine thing for poets and children, but not for locomotive drivers and I hope you and your fellow shop stewards share my views, Emrys.' The Colonel's smile vanished and he returned to the table and stubbed out his cigar. The worry was over, the problem was solved, and he had solved it. Billy Smith was a nut-case and Archie Vayne was the man of the moment. Colonel of Engineers, Senior Security Officer, every inch a commander. 'Driver Smith is in urgent need of psychiatric treatment and he must be suspended from duty immediately and indefinitely, Dr Puxton.'

'You're wrong, sir. You're completely and utterly wrong.' Edward Morcom had replaced the telephone and it was his turn to smile. His turn to humiliate a bullying superior and expose a pompous fool to the ridicule he deserved. 'Mr Smith saved countless lives by stopping that express and you can forget about ghosts and fairy tales and mental illness.' Morcom had taken notes of the telephone message and he held out his jotting pad for Vayne's inspection. 'A man did try to wreck the 9.15 last night and the police have just found him.'

Two

'Pretty nasty, isn't it, Colonel?' Inspector Thomas Mason of the Outer Croydon C.I.D. spoke thickly because he was sucking two cough lozenges to dull his sense of smell. 'The police surgeon considers that he died around midnight, but those brutes made a real meal of the blighter and they were still on the job when a patrolman spotted him. You can't blame that lad for being sick.'

'Decidedly nasty, Mr Mason, though I've seen worse sights in battle.' Archibald Vayne grimaced at the figure displayed on a mortuary trolley. 'No, you can't blame young Smith for feeling squeamish. It makes my stomach rumble a bit and I'm a pretty hard citizen.' He turned to a table and looked at the other things on display. The records of despair and mania ... the story of a man who had hated trains.

'But at least Smith thought that he recognized this.' Vayne tapped an object that might have appeared comical under less gruesome circumstances, and had probably been bought from a toy shop. A devil head-dress with garish colouring and horns sprouting from the plastic skull. 'Nobody could have recognized the chap himself Not even his wife, if he ever had one.' The Colonel picked up Mason's typed report and grimaced again, partly at what he read and partly from the stench of bile, decay and excrement that pervaded the room like gas compressed into a liquid.

The dead man's name was Sean Joseph Brady and he had been born in an Irish village thirty years ago, though few people knew that. His acquaintances in the doss houses and hostels and drop-out pads had called him the Late Horse and for two reasons. *Horse* because he was hooked on heroin and *Late* because he drank methylated spirit when he couldn't get a fix. Before the police discovered a drug addict's registration card in the breast pocket of his torn, bloodstained jacket, they thought the corpse had belonged to a man of seventy and their error was justifiable. Sean Brady was six feet tall, but he weighed less than six stone. His kidneys, lungs and liver were diseased, his hair was grey and he hadn't got a face under the hair; not much of a face. He had been dying of a heroin overdose when he collapsed on a stretch of wasteland near the railway and he hadn't died alone. Rats kept the Late Horse company and they'd eaten him alive.

'Surely we've seen enough, sir?' Edward Morcom was trying not to follow Billy Smith's example and vomit. 'The mask proves that Brady was the man Smith saw on the bridge. The letter and the haversack show that he hoped to sabotage the train and that settles the matter. Let's go back to the inspector's office, Colonel.'

'Is the matter settled, Ted?' Though Vayne had shared his assistant's discomfort and disgust, he was resisting nausea. 'I hope you're right. I hope to hell you're right, but *Ah hae mah doots* as my Scottish ancestors would have said.' He lowered the official report, tested the weight of the haversack Morcom had mentioned, and then thumbed through the photostat pages of a letter. 'Brady makes his intentions quite clear and he carried most of them out. He'd decided to wreck a train and he went about it carefully. He bought a devil mask to frighten the driver, he filled this bag with sleeper ballast and he dragged it up to the bridge. If the driver hadn't acted in time, Brady would have slung his home-made cannon ball at the cab windscreen and that might have been "Mission

27

accomplished" … a spectacular disaster … journey's end for Billy Smith and the 9.15.

'Fair enough, gentlemen, but could a man in Brady's mental state have planned such a scheme? Could a man in his physical state carry such a load? Would he have taken the bag away with him after the express stopped?'

'Dr Bevan thinks that he could have carried the sack, Colonel.' Inspector Mason was equally eager to get away from the horrible thing on the trolley and he glanced longingly at the door. 'According to Bevan, Brady would have been mentally and physically stimulated for approximately three-quarters of an hour after taking the overdose before the decline started, and it's anyone's guess why he didn't leave his missile on the bridge. Perhaps he hoped to make another sabotage attempt at a later date and use it again. Who can fathom the mind of a drugged, diseased maniac?'

'We can at least read what the maniac has written, Mr Mason, and I'm trying to read between his lines.' Vayne's eyes kept flicking from the photocopies to the corpse and he somehow knew that Morcom and the policeman were over-confident. 'This letter isn't only a statement of intended sabotage and murder. It's a suicide note and as phoney as your dummy teeth, Ted.' The Colonel knew that Morcom was sensitive about his dentures, but frustration as well as cruelty provoked the insult. The case was not closed, the mystery had not been solved, because something was wrong. Something was terribly wrong, but he didn't know what the thing was.

Apart from the mask and the haversack, the registration card and his soiled, shabby clothing, Sean Joseph Brady had had few possessions. Sixty-two pence, an empty hypodermic syringe, a half-empty bottle of meths, a ball-point pen and an envelope. A grimy envelope sealed with Sellotape which bore a non-existent address, but was crammed with information. The late Horse had hated trains and he'd expressed his hatred on sheets of toilet paper stolen from a station lavatory.

'Oh, Lord God, how I loathe them! Oh, sweet Jesus, give Your strength and Your blessing for what I have to do! Oh, sweet Virgin Mother Mary, have pity on me, a sinner.' The sloping, ill-formed letters were in keeping with Brady's character and background, and so was the preamble, Vayne thought. The ramblings of a deranged, superstitious Irish peasant whose brain had been rotted by heroin and raw alcohol. The statements which followed were also in character, if they were true. If the writer had really hated trains ... all trains. The mail train that had brought him to London, addiction and misery. The trains that roared past the pads and the hostels and disturbed his sleep. The trains carrying people to work when he was incapable of working. The trains that hurried people back to homes and families, and forward to holidays. Brady had no home and no family, and his only holidays came out of a bottle or the needle of a syringe.

All trains, but one train in particular. The only train on the system which was reserved for first-class passengers: the evening Channel Belle to Lythborne – the 9.15.

'Blessed Mary Mother of God, pity me and hold me in Your arms when I enter Your kingdom, which will not be long. My plans are laid and I crave for death, but give me the Power of Your grace as well as the strength of my main-line drug. The power to bear my cross to the bridge and end my nightmare. To wreck the monsters that are gnawing my soul.'

'Brady's intentions and mental state are lucid enough and his main-line shot did give him the necessary strength, though he failed to get his target – a main-line train.' Vayne lowered the last photocopy and smiled. 'Mr Sean Brady killed himself with a heroin overdose while the balance of his mind was disturbed, and driver William Smith is to be complimented for his prompt action. The case is over, gentlemen, so should we leave our dear departed brother in peace?

'Like hell we will!' The Inspector had opened the door, Morcom was hurrying after him, but Vayne's voice bellowed contemptuously and he strode to the trolley and bent over the corpse, probing the mangled flesh with his finger. 'This chap may or may not have killed himsell deliberately, and he may or may not have hoped to deraif the express. But he damned well didn't write that letter and I'll tell you why.' He crossed to a washbasin and turned on the taps. 'I don't claim to be a specialist in calligraphy, but I've got a pair of eyes in my head.' He grinned at Mason and Morcom while he washed his hands.

'And so have you, gentlemen, though you've forgotten how to use them. Take a look at the chap's arms, Inspector, and then ask your Super to assemble a murder squad. The rats stripped a lot of the flesh away, but the hypo-dermic punctures are still visible and those marks prove my point.' His smile widened as Mason took his place at the trolley. 'This swan song ... this crazy hymn of hate, might have been composed by our pal Brady, but Brady couldn't have written it. According to your own expert, a right-handed person penned this, and that lets out Sean Brady.' Vayne dried himself and returned to the photostat letter. 'He used the needle on his right arm and that's all the evidence you need.

'Q.E.D., Ted? What has been demonstrated, Inspector Mason?' He smiled again as the policeman nodded to Morcom. 'Mr Sean bloody Brady was left-handed.'

'We've got a hard one, Ted, so keep quiet and let me think.' After leaving Inspector Mason, Vayne and Morcom had returned to their office and the Colonel was studying a map and a folder of notes. 'Better still, make yourself useful and fetch me a drink, a very large Scotch with very little water. I'm trying to read the mind of a crazy saboteur and put myself in the place of a doped Irish drop-out. Difficult roles for a man like me, and alcohol might stimulate the imagination.' He watched Morcom unlock a filing cabinet labelled CLASSIFIED INFORMATION – SENIOR SUPERINTENDENT ONLY and take out a whisky bottle, and then closed his eyes for a moment.

Why? he wondered. Why should anybody want to wreck a train? Easy questions with several answers: insanity, vandalism, the sheer love of destruction. Also political terrorism, though that could be ruled out in this instance. If the I.R.A. had intended to sabotage the 9.15, they'd have done the job properly. No messing about with a bag of rocks to stun or kill the engine crew. The brave sons of Erin would have planted a bomb on the line and lists of the dead and injured would be published already.

No, not the I.R.A. nor any other political organization. The whole affair had appeared amateurish and sloppy and if Vayne hadn't been clever enough to see that Brady's letter was a forgery the authorities might have dismissed the matter as a bungled attempt by a single, embittered lunatic.

Which was what the real saboteur wanted them to think, of course, though Vayne couldn't imagine why. If Brady had been illiterate he might have dictated the message to a friend, but that was not likely. After Vayne spotted the deception, Mr Mason had telephoned a Salvation Army hostel and been assured that Brady could write clearly and grammatically.

'Thanks.' Morcom had put a glass on his desk and Vayne knocked back half its contents in a single practised movement before considering his second role, which was equally easy. If Sean Brady was craving for a fix as usual,

31

some kind person might have offered him one in return for certain favours. 'I want you to fill this haversack with ballast and carry it to the bridge by the Crematorium. When you reach the bridge, you will station yourself over the fast line and wait till you see the Lythborne express approaching.' A hypodermic syringe had glinted, its needle had dug into a phial and the tempter's conditions had been amplified and accepted. Sean Joseph Brady had lurched happily away with his shot and his sack and his devil head-dress and he'd never suspected that the shot was a lethal dose designed to kill him. He'd felt top-o'-the-mornin' when he put on the plastic cap and raised his missile over the parapet, and the fact that the train stopped wouldn't have distressed him. The drug would have kept him happy and he'd walked on till he reached the stretch of wasteland and collapsed, dying of heroin poisoning and probably too weak to scream when the rats got their teeth into him. Regarded as a deranged *saboteur manqué* if it hadn't been for the cleverness of Colonel Archie Vayne.

'No – no – no.' Vayne spoke aloud and cupped his chin on his fist like a grotesque parody of Rodin's *Thinker*. 'It's wrong, Ted. It's all bloody wrong. Not even the most inept plotter would rely on Brady, and that haversack weighed thirty-three pounds. The man would never have carried such a load away with him. He'd have dumped it on the track or left it lying in the gutter. You and I have to stop talking nonsense and do some serious brain work.' He glared at Morcom who hadn't uttered a syllable for at least ten minutes.

'Brady was just a fall-guy, a scapegoat, and he never had the haversack or the head-dress. All his obliging friend gave him was an injection of dope and a letter to deliver. An envelope addressed to a house at the other side of the wasteland which was demolished years ago. Brady couldn't have known that the address no longer existed, but his

32

friend had told him the route to take and the friend knew that he'd collapse before reaching the demolition site. The friend knew where to find his dead scapegoat, *after* the accident.'

'I'm sorry, sir, but I'm not with you.' Vayne had stressed the word *after* and Morcom frowned. 'You're implying that another man tried to derail the train and then planted the evidence on Brady's body, the mask and the haversack and a written confession. A clever, logical alibi, but a poor attempt at sabotage which failed through incompetence. The work of a child or a compulsive lunatic.'

'Children can be as logical as Aristotle, Ted, and there's method in madness.' Vayne finished the rest of his whisky and held out the glass for a refill. 'You're right about compulsive lunacy though, because if our chap had succeeded, the crash would have been an exact replica of the earlier one. Same train, same date and time, same location – the Crem curve.

'Also the son of the driver who was crippled in the first crash, which suggests that our villain has an obsession against a train or a family. Someone who knew that Billy Smith would be driving the Belle last night. Someone employed by the railway.

'And maybe someone who intended to fail and Brady's murder is an insurance policy for the future. Our loonie must have suspected that young Smith would be tense and anxious when he pulled out of the terminus; thinking of his father ... watching the bridge and ready to jam on the brakes and reverse the motors if he saw anyone on the parapet. Yesterday's performance could be just a preview for the real curtain-raiser, because Smith won't be anxious next time he's in charge of the 9.15. At least he wouldn't be, if I hadn't spotted the deception. He'd think that Brady was the prime mover and Brady killed himself. The danger is past, the mystery is solved and Dad is revenged. Smith can climb confidently into the locomotive and let her rip. When he does there'll be an exact reproduction of what happened three years ago.'

'Not exact, sir.' Morcom returned with the glass. 'William Smith's father said that he saw two people on the bridge: a boy and a girl. Smith himself noticed only one: a boy or a man wearing the devil head-dress.'

'Old Smith wasn't sure what he saw, Ted, and he was unconscious for several days after the accident.' Though Vayne realized Morcom had raised an important point, he didn't believe in complimenting minions. 'It doesn't matter a damn whether one or two individuals are involved because forewarned is forearmed and I'm armed to the teeth. I know that there'll be more attacks on that train before a week's out. I can feel it burning in my guts.' He heated the organs with a further gulp of Scotch. 'And when the next attack comes, I'll be ready and waiting to nail the swine.

'But there's something I've forgotten.' A sudden recollection made the Colonel belch like an unblocked drain and he reached for the file. 'Before the telephone call about Brady interrupted us, Billy Smith was making a statement, and he named the figure on the bridge by name. "Poor Simple Simon our dead brother."

'Simple Simon, that's got a nice, sinister ring, but who is he? A hooligan who smashes things, a maniac escaped from an asylum, a figment of the imagination? I don't know, but I intend to pay a social visit and find out.' He pushed the file over for Morcom's inspection. 'Unless this data is incomplete, we've got another loonie to worry about and that loonie lied to me less than two hours ago.' He looked at his watch and stood up. 'Billy Smith never had a brother.'

Three

'You're certain that Billy used the name Simple Simon, Colonel Vayne?' Mrs Dorothy Smith stood with her back to a rosewood sideboard which was so highly polished that it resembled tinted glass. 'Poor Billy, he really has got a load on his mind. Simon is dead and we don't talk about him any more.

'But thank you for telling me this, and thank you for all you have done. If you hadn't noticed that that Irishman was left-handed, the police would have closed the case and let our persecution continue. Now at least we're forewarned and deeply in your debt.'

'Not at all, Madam. I merely carried out a job of work and kept my wits about me.' Vayne smiled modestly at the woman who was looking at him with what he imagined to be a mixture of admiration, awe and gratitude. A most intelligent and attractive woman, though her hair was grey, there was a hint of wrinkles under her thick make-up and the blue eyes behind her glasses showed strain and unhappiness. 'But, I'm afraid I don't quite understand what you mean by persecution, Mrs Smith. Are you implying that the attacks were directed against your husband and your son rather than the train?'

'I'll tell you what I believe in a moment, but please make yourself comfortable and let me get you a drink first.' She turned to open the sideboard. 'What would you care for?'

'A Scotch and water would be most welcome.' Vayne lowered himself into a sofa and glanced around the room.

Apart from the woman's statements there were several things he did not understand: the neighbourhood, the house and the telephone. He had called without making an appointment because Peter Smith was not listed in the directory, but there was a phone on the window-ledge. He had expected that the Smiths would live in a council flat or a terrace house in some working-class district teeming with bustle and children and coloured immigrants. But his map had led him to the exact opposite. A pocket of upper-crust suburbia: detached, Regency-style residences with two-car garages and wide lawns and flower gardens. A very select and quiet pocket where children did not play in the streets and the neighbours kept themselves to themselves, except for polite greetings on their way to and from the shops and the station.

Most unexpected, and his hostess was the most unexpected factor of all. Colonel Vayne had forgotten her maiden name till she opened the door, but he recognized her background as soon as she spoke and told him that her husband and children were out. Archie Vayne was a snob and he knew a lady when he saw one.

'My dictionary describes persecution as maltreatment and harassment, Colonel, and that is why I used the term.' She had poured out a generous measure of whisky and carried the glass to an occasional table at his side. 'Some person, or more probably several persons, are persecuting my family and their aim is destruction, physical and mental. They wish to cripple and kill or drive us mad.' She spoke without the slightest trace of emotion and her hand was quite steady as she lowered the glass. 'Have I given you enough water, Colonel?'

'This is perfect, Madam.' Archie Vayne sampled the drink indifferently. Though he rarely refused a Scotch, he was more interested in information than alcohol and he wouldn't have complained if she had offered him a mug of cocoa. 'Have you any idea who these people are, or why they wish to harm you?'

'God knows who they are, or rather the Devil knows, and I hope that you will be able to find out.' She walked back to the sideboard and mixed herself a gin and vermouth. 'But there are many possible answers to your second question and it might help if I told you a story. A fairy story with a conventional beginning.' She smiled and raised her glass. 'Once upon a time there was a poor, lonely princess who imagined that a churlish peasant was a king in disguise.

'No, that's wrong.' Mrs Smith hesitated and Vayne saw that she herself was wrong. The calm, unemotional manner was a sham, the eyes behind her spectacles were terrified and she was struggling to control a nervous tic trembling on the left cheek of her still young and attractive face. Mrs Peter Smith, *née* the Hon. Dorothy Callington-Graves, was fighting to stop her whole body shaking and if she'd been alone she would probably have wept or screamed aloud.

'There were two lonely princesses, Colonel Vayne, and a nursery rhyme describes their flight far better than a fairy tale. I can show you some illustrations of the rhyme, if you'd care to see them.' She took a heavy, leather-bound volume from a bookshelf and handed it to Vayne before sitting down beside him and tapping her glass against his. 'Cheers, Colonel.

'Those are the pictures, but what are the words? I keep forgetting.' She frowned while he opened the book and then nodded. 'Yes, I remember now. A silly song for silly children.

'Once a lady loved a swine ... "Humph," said he.
"Oh, Piggy dear, will you be mine?" "Humph," said he.

37

'Not a very poetic ditty, Colonel, but I hope you'll agree that the illustrations contain elements of romance and tragedy.' She smiled at Vayne's expression, a forced, neurotic smile with no humour or joy in it. 'The lady did love her swine, you see. The tragedy is that she still loves him.'

The book was a photograph album. The photographs were snapshots of two families and two marriages, and both families had produced fools and knaves. The story contained no romance or tragedy in Vayne's opinion and he started to despise his hostess before she was half-way through her confession. A squalid tale of lust, delinquency and betrayal of class.

Mrs Dottie Smith (the Hon. Dorothy Sylvia Callington-Graves as she'd been christened) and her sister, Janet, were the daughters of decent upper-class parents and they'd been given decent upbringings and decent educations. Why had they crawled into the gutter and married louts? Vayne looked at three exhibits. An imposing Victorian country mansion, a squalid back-to-back terrace house facing a railway siding, a scruffy, long-haired man brandishing a red banner. Janet Callington-Graves had fallen for an unbalanced Anarchist she met at a Hyde Park rally and after fourteen years of matrimony they'd made a suicide pact in protest against mankind's inhumanity to man. The only satisfactory thing was that the pact had been honoured and mankind had lost some very bad rubbish.

And, although sister Dorothy suffered from no moral or political aberrations, she'd been just as foolish and perverse and tainted. Her parents were quite right to disown her, but what a shame that they hadn't changed their wills before taking a much-needed holiday and dying in an aircraft disaster. Two more photographs aroused the Colonel's

pity and revulsion. A handsome middle-aged couple strid-
ing across a grouse moor with shotguns at the ready; a boy
and a girl guzzling candyfloss in a fairground. The boy
had a slogan, 'I'm the Greatest' embroidered on his
singlet. The girl, easily recognizable as Mrs Smith, sported
a similar vulgarism on her over-tight sweater: 'Pete is my
king.'

Disgusting, Vayne thought. If that was the best that
breeding, money and education could do, God help the
country.

'I never completed my education, Colonel.' The woman
appeared to be a bit of a mind reader and she smiled at his
expression. 'Peter Smith and I were married on my eighteenth birthday and how happy we were at first. The lady
worshipped her swine, and she tried to model herself on
him. She didn't even mind when he got drunk on his days
off and knocked her about. If you're married yourself you
may be able to appreciate my feelings. The craving to
become part of another person, body and soul. To ignore
convention and laugh at hostility.'

'Afraid I'm a widower, Mrs Smith. Wife died some years
back. Very sad and tragic loss ... still miss her.' The
Colonel lied glibly. Pam's loss was his gain and he never
missed her. He had certainly never wanted to become part
of her, and he'd never had the courage to knock her about,
though the notion was enjoyable. But he had to gain
Dorothy Smith's confidence and he reached out and
patted her arm sympathetically. 'Know what you mean,
however. "Let not against the union of true minds admit
impediment." '

'Exactly.' The quotation was inaccurate, but she seemed
pleased by his sentiments. 'There were impediments, of
course. My father and mother despised Peter and they
only met him once, which was understandable. Pete had
a chip on his shoulder and when Daddy offered to help

39

him better himself, he lost his temper and swore at them. He said that there was more dignity in driving a train than lolling back in company Rolls-Royces with a bunch of idle, fat-arsed company directors. He said that those snorting locos were his life and I suppose they were; proud, foolish, headstrong Peter.' Vayne had reached a section of the book devoted to the Smith family's career and she frowned at the illustrations: drivers and trains and railway engines. An arrogant, bearded man leaning out of the cab of a Schools class locomotive. A Battle of Britain Pacific blowing off steam in Trafalgar Road Terminus. The Channel Belle roaring down to Lythborne behind a Deltic diesel.

'I realized that my own people might disapprove of our marriage, but I didn't suspect that the others would resent it. Peter's own parents were dead – some virus infection that the doctor didn't diagnose in time – but he had friends and neighbours and workmates, and how they disliked me! I didn't mind so much till the children were born: my daughter, Betty, in '55 and Billy a year later. I put up with their sneers about Lady Chatterley's Lover and Madam Head-in-Air, but when they started on the kids, I could have strangled the bastards.

'I tried to fit in, Colonel Vayne. I tried to become part of Pete's community and think like 'em. I even tried to speak like 'em. I tried so bleedin' hard.' A trace of cockney joined her crisp, cultured accent. 'But it was no good. They never accepted us and Pete didn't help matters. Pete was furious when the headmaster said that Bill should try for a scholarship to Oxford, and he tore up one of Betty's paintings after she was offered a place at the National College of Design. Peter believed that what was good enough for him and his family was good enough for our children, and that's why Billy has to drive trains and Bet slaves away in a factory. The working-class image had to be preserved and Peter wouldn't even let me buy a decent home with the money I got from my father's estate. Not till his train left the rails and crippled him.

'What a waste of talent, Colonel. Our Billy should have gone to the university. My Betty might have been such a fine artist.' She pointed at an oil painting on the wall which Vayne had already noticed. Five people sunbathing on a beach against a background of hills and palm trees and little white houses. Mrs Smith and her husband were sitting in deck chairs with their children standing behind them. Vayne recognized Billy Smith, and the daughter bore a striking resemblance to her mother. But he didn't recognize the younger boy seated in the third chair with a plumed Red Indian war bonnet on his head. A handsome boy; his features were firm and even, his lips smiled and his bright, blue eyes seemed to shine from the canvas like light bulbs.

Eyes which were too bright and too sharp. The sharpest eyes Archie Vayne had ever seen and he'd met some sharp characters in his time. Eyes with the same pleading quality which reminded him of Billy Smith and another boy whose name he couldn't remember. Private ... Corporal ... Sergeant Thingummyjig? Cadet ... Lieutenant Something-or-other? The boy who had shot himself.

'Betty painted that on our last holiday in Spain, Colonel.' Mrs Smith's own blue eyes were riveted on the painting. 'Don't you think it shows talent?'

'Afraid I don't know much about art, dear lady. Just a simple soldier, but I do know what I like and I definitely like that.' The next lies were equally glib because Archie Vayne was far from simple and he did not like the picture. Though the general conception was sentimental and mawkish, there was something sinister about the man and the boy in the chairs. There was something suspicious about the whole Smith family and he became more and more convinced that the 9.15 was a secondary target and the saboteur's real venom was directed against Billy and his father. He also suspected that his hostess had guessed who the saboteur might be and it was time to come into the open.

'Yes, in my untrained opinion that painting shows great talent, and it's a pity that your daughter didn't take up art as a career.' Vayne had been told that Betty Smith worked for A.C.I.D., *Allied Chemical Industrial Developments*, which virtually belonged to Sir Solomon Kahn. Good, old Solly; former school friend, fellow club member and a man he enjoyed baiting. 'It's also a shame that Billy didn't go to university, but it's your other son who interests me.' Vayne finished the whisky and his tone changed. The friendly manner vanished and his voice became harsh and hectoring. 'This lad with a fondness for fancy dress.' He stood up and scowled at the Indian war bonnet on the canvas. 'Why didn't you register his birth and why did you say, "We don't talk about him any more"?

'Simple Simon?' Vayne sneered the name. 'Was he so simple that he went potty after a while and had to be locked away in a madhouse? Did you lie to your other children because you're ashamed of mania, Mrs Smith? Did you tell Billy that his brother was dead when he was alive and kicking in a padded cell? If that's the case you've got a lot to answer for, because Simon's out of his cell and on the rampage.' The Colonel swung round and saw that his bullying attitude was bearing fruit. The woman's nervous tic had become more pronounced and tears were trickling from under her glasses. 'I didn't believe Billy when he told me that he saw the ghost of his brother on the bridge. But I'm beginning to believe him now, because the ghost likes wearing funny hats. He enjoys wrecking trains and persecuting people. He murdered Sean Brady the other night and there'll be more murders unless you help me.

42

'Yes, our persecution continues.' Vayne mimicked the woman's voice. 'That's what you said, Mrs Smith, and I think you know who's responsible for the persecution. An insane son who's either escaped or been released from an asylum.'

'We only had one son, Colonel, and Simon's dead. If you don't believe me, go and ask me husband at the local boozer.' The false cockney accent as well as the tic had become stronger and her words twanged harshly around the room. 'Yers, go along to the King's Arms and ask the King himself, the lout I married. If Billy saw Simon on the bridge, he saw a ghost. The ghost of a poor, unhappy boy we all loved, the prince who left us.

'The boozer's at the end of Maypole Street and yer'll find Peter in the public bar if yer hurry.' She glanced at her watch and opened the door. 'Peter, the King, will tell you about Simple Simon, Colonel Vayne. Our prince is dead and the King's pride killed 'im.'

Four

'Twenty-six ... Twenty-seven and a half ... twenty-eight.'
The King sat in the public bar of the King's Arms, a-
counting out his money. 'Twenty-nine pence. That's the
price of me pint, Mister, and if you'll fetch it for me I'll be
obliged.' Peter Smith pushed a pile of change across the
table and watched Vayne pick it up and walk to the
counter. He'd been tempted to accept the Colonel's offer
to buy him a drink, but *no thank you*. He had his pride and
his rules and he observed those rules as strictly as he'd
once observed the time schedules. Three pints of bitter was
his ration and he went to the pub with the exact amount
of money to pay for them. Nobody was going to say that
old Peter Smith was a lush or a cadger. No one could make
old Pete lose his self-control.

Old Peter! Poor, old Peter Smith, the deposed King.
Though he was only forty-four, age is relative. He felt old
and he was old: old and crippled and damn-near blind.
Both his legs had been crushed when the 9.15 left the rails,
and though the surgeons had done their best and he didn't
need the wheelchair or the crutches, he still walked with a
limp and stairs troubled him. His left arm was partially
paralysed, he kept his peaked cap pulled down to try to
hide the scar tissue mottling his forehead and he wore
tinted glasses because his optic nerve had been affected
and even dim lighting made his eyes smart. He was a
wreck and a has-been, a drone living on his pension and
Dorothy's money.

'Ta, Mister.' He grunted as Vayne returned with their
drinks. 'Now, what was you asking me before Maureen

interrupted us?' He nodded at the barmaid who had delivered a telephone message from his daughter to say that she would call at the pub on her way back from work and drive him home.

'Aye, I remember, though me memory's as faulty as me body. You want to know about Simon, and our Bill told us who you were. Your name's Vile and you're a junior accident inspector who thought Bill was a nut-case. A stupid neurotic who was so obsessed with ... with ... ' He paused and took a swig of beer. 'So concerned with what happened to me three years ago that he started to imagine things and stopped the train in panic.

'But you were wrong, weren't you, Mr Inspector Vile? You've had to swallow your words and eat humble pie. There was someone on the Crem Bridge and if my son hadn't kept his wits about him, there'd have been another derailment for you and your superiors to investigate. The Irishman's murder proves there's a saboteur at work and a bloody cunning one. That's why you've come to me cap in hand, Mr Vile.'

'My name is Lieutenant-Colonel Archibald Vayne, Smith, and I hold the post of Senior Security Superintendent.' The man's tone was mocking and though Vayne couldn't see through the dark lenses he was sure that the eyes behind them were twinkling with malice. Dorothy Smith had been right in saying that she'd married a swine and others shared her opinion. Emrys Evans knew several men who'd worked with the self-styled King of the Road and the verdict was unanimous. 'A sodding big-mouth who thought he owned the sodding Channel Belle.' 'Thought he owned the whole sodding railway, because his father and grandfather had worked on it all their sodding lives.' 'Gave his missus merry hell and stopped his sodding kids going to college.' 'Didn't want 'em to do better than 'imself – the sodding bastard.'

45

'Only a *lieutenant*-colonel, sir? The chap who investigated my case was a full colonel; not that his rank did me any good.' The mockery increased and then vanished abruptly as though a mask had been torn from the scarred face. 'Sorry, Super, I admit I was riling you, but don't blame me for being bitter. Three years back some bastards smashed me and me train and now they're trying to do the same thing to our Billy.

'Why, Colonel Vayne? Why should people hate us? The neighbours and me mates laughing because I married a rich man's daughter and that man regarded me as dirt. My wife wanting to move out and buy a house in some toffee-nosed suburb, like we've got now, and how I loathe it. Billy and Betty grumbling because I wouldn't let 'em go to college and university. Simon running away from school because a few kids bullied him.' Smith knocked back more beer and banged the glass on the table. 'Why did everyone criticize me, sir? Is it wrong for Billy to be a driver like his Dad and his grandfather and his great-grandfather? Why shouldn't Betty work in a factory, same as me Mum did? We're working-class stock. There's nought wrong with honest toil, and though I wedded a lah-de-dah lass I treated her well. I even gave young Simon a home and what good came of it? He cleared off and killed himself.

'Simon was no son of mine, sir, though I suppose Bill and Betty regarded him as a brother.' Smith had frowned at Vayne's next question. 'We all tried to make Simon Lent feel he was one of us, and it wasn't our fault that we failed. Not Simon's fault either, I suppose, and you've got to give the devil his due.

'Ta, Colonel.' He had taken a cigarette from a crumpled packet and leaned forward when Vayne held out his lighter. 'Simon Lent was my sister-in-law's child and she sent him to some cranky boarding school where the kids

46

were supposed to learn self-discipline. A fat lot of comfort that discipline must have been after he came home on holiday and saw his parents lying naked together in a bath. Naked and dead, sir. The selfish fools had cut their wrists with a razor blade and they'd been rotting there for a week before Simon found 'em.

'No, you can't blame young Simon for being a bit peculiar; maybe suicide was in his blood, but I don't know what made him decide to run away, because I wasn't there. I was runnin' meself.' He inhaled deeply and then closed his eyes to picture that run. His last run on the Channel Belle which had ended in darkness.

Three years and two days ago, and thirteen minutes lost because of a points failure at the terminus. Almost a quarter of an hour, but what did that matter to him ... to Peter Smith, the King of the Road? The signals turned to green, the night was fine and clear and a big, white moon had seemed to smile and urge him on. On over the Thames and up along the incline with the motors pounding and singing as his speed increased and the locomotive surged forward. Sixty ... seventy ... eighty miles an hour and the throttle wide open. On to Lythborne – on to regain lost time. On through the London suburbs and then down to the Crem and the Crem Bridge with the restriction sign heralding the curve beyond it. On to the figure or figures leaning over the bridge. On to the rock that had crashed against the windscreen and thrown him down with his hand still clutching the throttle lever. Down and on to the floor of the cab with the wheels bucketing across the ballast till they reached the embankment and darkness came. Down on to a hospital bed with tubes attached to his body and his mind drugged and barely conscious. Sometimes he'd known that Dot was with him, stroking his cheek and murmuring endearments, but he couldn't reply to her or take in what she was saying. He had to

47

concentrate on the past and it was all so vague and shadowy. What had Simon told him on the morning before the accident? What had he said to Billy and Betty before leaving for work? Unpleasant recollections, but they faded after a while and worse was to come ... far worse.

'I was in that blasted hospital for five months before the doctors said they'd patched me up as well as they could and allowed me to go home.' He spoke more to himself than to Vayne. 'But it wasn't our home; not that snug little house in Sunderland Terrace where we'd lived together, me and Dot, the kids and Simon. I thought that ambulance men had made a mistake when they drew up at that great, snobby place you've just come from, sir. I didn't understand a thing till they wheeled me chair into the hall and Dot showed me our fan mail and explained what those bastards had been doing.' He reached in his breast pocket and produced a wad of yellowing papers held together by an elastic band.

'Have a look at that mail, sir. Though I couldn't attend the court of enquiry, the president decided that a rock had hit the cab and I was exonerated of all blame and given a pension. But some people blamed me and they took it out on my family while I was lying helpless in that bloody ward.' He slipped off the band and laid the papers on the table. 'See for yourself, Colonel. That's why Dot had to leave Sunderland Terrace and use the money her father left her to buy a house out here. That's why our phone number is not listed in the directory. It could also explain what Billy saw the other night.'

'Your last statement is unlikely, Mr Smith, and almost every driver, airline pilot and ship's officer involved in a major disaster receives filth of this kind. The world is full of vicious lunatics.' Vayne flocked through the papers which failed to impress him because he'd seen similar exhibits before; anonymous letters full of spite, accusations and threats. For example: 'My father died on the 9.15, Smith, because you were drunk or incompetent and I shall curse you for the rest of your life.' 'May God the Avenger pursue you through eternity.' 'You don't know me, Mrs Smith, but I know you and your children and they'll pay for what your husband did.'

'But it wasn't just the letters. Not just loonies who hadn't the guts to sign their names.' Peter Smith had noticed Vayne's lack of interest and a trace of his earlier hostility returned. 'How would you like your missus to be stopped in the street by neighbours and told that she'd married a murderer or a crazy suicide who'd wrecked his train deliberately? To have a brick slung through her window and shopkeepers refusing to serve her? To be scared stiff whenever the phone rang, because there might be a sadistic nut on the end of the line? Could you tolerate that, sir?'

'Of course not, and I naturally appreciate why your family had to move.' Though Archie Vayne was trying to concentrate on the case, some personal thoughts had occurred to him and he stifled a smile. How would Pam have reacted if their Mayfair neighbours had insulted her in public? What would she have said if the staff of Harrods or Fortnum and Mason had refused to serve her? Would a few abusive phone calls have punctured her self-esteem? Verbal humiliation of Pam was an attractive notion, but bricks were even better. He'd have enjoyed seeing a brick shatter Pam's window, providing he wasn't in the firing line himself.

'You're suggesting that someone who suffered on account of your accident may have dreamed up a vendetta against your son, Mr Smith, but I think that's unlikely.' The images of his wife's discomforts faded and Vayne returned to duty. Though the pub was filling up, two voices in his brain drowned the conversations and the laughter and the orders for drinks. A boy's voice and the voice of a woman. 'That's who was standing on the bridge … Poor Simple Simon, our dead brother.' 'Our prince is dead and the King's pride killed him.'

'Billy imagined that he recognized the man he saw the other night, and I want to know about that man, Mr Smith. Simon Lent, whom you and your wife adopted as your own child … who became part of the family.'

'There's not much to tell, sir. The lad drowned himself in Australia and he's best forgotten.' Smith lowered his eyes as though fearing that Vayne might be able to see through the thick, tinted lenses and read the thoughts behind them. 'Nay, that's a lie. There's plenty to tell and we'll never forget Simon. He's haunted the lot of us and maybe that's why Bill believed he saw the poor, wretched little devil.' He looked up and finished the rest of his beer. 'I'm going to break my rule and have a drink on you, Colonel, and then I'll tell you what I know about the boy they called Simple Simon.' There was a fireplace near the table and he leaned forward and massaged his hands before the glowing anthracite as Vayne crossed to the bar. One crippled hand and one good hand that had betrayed him. If his fingers had released the throttle the brakes would have been applied automatically and stopped the train long before it reached the bend and disaster.

'That's very kind of you, sir.' Vayne had returned with another mug of beer and he straightened and smiled at him. 'It didn't take you long to get served, but I suppose those stuck-up bitches behind the counter can recognize a toff and gave you preference.

'Just like the teachers at Glendale Road Comprehensive gave Simon Lent preference.' He raised the glass and drank deeply. 'Simple Simon! A damned stupid nickname because the boy was as bright as they come. Brighter than

Billy and Betty put together and the headmaster said he was wasted at Glendale Road and advised my wife to send him to a public school. Too bright in class and too attractive to the girls with his baby-blue eyes and snobby manners. That's why the other lads hated his guts and kept knocking him about. Why he used to come home in tears and beg to be transferred somewhere else.

'They all wanted that, Colonel. The teachers and my own wife and children supported Simon Lent, but I don't hold with private education and I wouldn't have it. Billy and Betty had a rough passage when they first went to Glendale, but they're tough like me and they stood up for themselves. The other kids soon learned to leave 'em alone, and I thought it would be the same with Simon. That he'd change his damned accent and learn to be a man ... a man like me.

'Was I wrong to make him stay at Glendale Road, sir?' Smith's hand trembled as he raised the beer mug and he didn't wait for Vayne to answer the question. 'Was it my fault that the little weakling ran away on the day of me accident and went to Sydney as a ship's steward? I did what I thought was best for Simon, Colonel, and we belted a couple of the louts who'd been hounding him, Billy and me. Waited for 'em outside the school one night, and though I can't remember their names, they'll not forget us in a hurry. We gave them a proper hiding and they swore blind that they'd never lay a finger on Simon again.

'So why did he clear off, sir? Why did he have to go to Australia and kill himself?'

'How can you be sure that he did kill himself?' Vayne knew that the man was desperate for assurance, but his feelings were unimportant and he had some questions of his own to answer. Peter Smith was an arrogant despot who had forced his adopted child to remain at a school where he was persecuted. Simon Lent must have hated

Smith for that, so had he run away to sea before the police asked where he was and what he was doing on the night the Belle crashed?

A possible solution, but there were others. Peter and Billy Smith had waylaid two of Lent's persecutors and roughed them up. Could those persecutors have resented their punishment and planned a revenge far more bitter than any beating? Glendale Road was near the railway locomotive sheds and many of its pupils would be railwaymen's children who'd know that Peter Smith would be in charge of the 9.15. How easy and simple to drop a rock from the bridge. What fun to wreck a train and kill its driver, a man who had assaulted them. A brutal boaster whom their parents resented; Peter Smith, the self-styled King of the Road.

And what about the recent event? Could schoolboys cherish hatred for three years and decide to attack again? To destroy the son as well as the father, and plan the attack so expertly; forging a letter, obtaining an overdose of heroin and using Brady as a scapegoat?

No, too complicated and too well planned. As untenable as his earlier notion that Billy really had seen Simon Lent on the bridge. It was much more likely that the saboteur was a deranged adult. A man who had been injured or bereaved by the first wreck and hoped to reproduce the events that had ruined him. That was a far more probable explanation Vayne thought, and Smith confirmed his view, fumbling in his breast pocket and producing another sheet of faded paper.

'Simon Lent killed himself all right, Colonel, and here's the proof. Simon wrote a suicide letter stating exactly what he intended to do.' He held the exhibit out for Vayne's inspection. 'Simon's mates on the ship hounded him worse than the school kids and he couldn't take no more bullying. He'd decided to chuck himself into Sydney

52

harbour, and if Bill saw him on that bridge he must have been looking at a bleedin' ghost. Read what he wrote and then tell me I'm a liar, sir.'

'You're not a liar, Mr Smith, but you've got poor eyesight.' Vayne was frowning at the page and it wasn't the contents that made him frown, the disjointed complaints of misery and the admissions of defeat. Simon Lent had realized he attracted hatred like a magnet tugs at iron, and death was the only door to release him from hell. Very sad and tragic, but it was the writing that interested Archie Vayne. Sloping, uneven handwriting which he'd seen on another suicide note and it fascinated him so much that he didn't realize he and Smith had company and someone was standing behind him. Someone who had overheard the end of their conversation. He didn't look at the girl till she snatched the paper from his grasp, though Betty Smith was worth looking at. Slim, blonde and beautiful; rather like her mother must have been before her hair went grey and worry and sadness produced wrinkles on the still youthful face and around the haunted eyes.

'I dunno who yer friend is, Dad, but yer've bin talkin' crap and that letter's a pack of lies. Our Billy didn't see no ghost the other evenin', and I'll tell yer why.' The mother's face, but not the mother's voice. Peter Smith had knocked the lah-de-dah out of his kids and Betty's accent was broad cockney.

'Or rather I'll ask yer why. Can ghosts lift receivers and dial numbers? Can dead men speak on telephones?' Before Vayne could stop her she crumpled the paper into a ball and threw it on the fire. 'Well, Simon Lent can use a blower, Dad, and I've just bin listenin' to 'im.'

Five

'If we're right, Billy ... if you did see Simon ... if it was his voice I heard on the telephone, he's got it in for us; for all of us.' Though the room was warm and brightly lit, Betty Smith felt numb with cold and her sight seemed to be failing. An icy mist had formed around her eyes – she was wearing dark glasses like Dad's – she was as tired and defeated as Mum, and she looked at the blurred figures of her parents seated by the electric fire and shivered. If only Dad was as strong and commanding as he had been before that accident, that attempt to murder him. If only Mum could realize the danger and advise her. If only Simon had spoken more distinctly. If only her head would stop aching and allow her to think clearly.

So many *if onlys*, but it was no good complaining about the past. She'd been dazed and angry when she reached the King's Arms and a reflex action had made her snatch that false, lying letter from Colonel Vayne and throw it on to the fire. She had hardly realized that Vayne was a railway official after Dad introduced them, but she'd seen that Dad was as distressed as herself and one of his bad turns was starting. Dad had to be got home quickly, so she'd asked Vayne to excuse them and hurried Dad out of the bar.

How right she was. Betty walked over to her father and fondled his left hand. A warm hand with a steady pulse beating in the wrist, but there was no response to her touch. The nerves were virtually useless and the brain behind the scarred forehead had ceased to register.

Though Dad's eyes were open and looking towards her, Betty knew that they were not looking *at* her. Dad had been disturbed by Vayne's statements and her own statements had worried him even more. Dad was far away from the warm, comfortable room and he'd withdrawn from reality. The years had slipped back and Dad was speeding down to Lythborne on the 9.15, watching the signals and the control panels and the rails gleaming in the moonlight. He'd watched everything he was supposed to watch, but nobody had told him to watch the bridge and he'd sped on towards it and only caught a glimpse of the figure crouched over the parapet before the rock fell and his windscreen shattered. Poor Dad hadn't anticipated the earlier attack and he was trying to dismiss the present threat now. Dozing away in his dream world, oblivious of what she and Billy were saying and only partially conscious of Mum seated at his side.

Poor Dad ... Poor Mum. They would never recover from the wreck of the 9.15. They refused to accept that there might be an even worse wreck unless Simon Lent was appeased.

'We're not imagining things, Billy. You saw his face and I heard his voice. Simon Lent is alive and kicking; kicking at me.' Betty turned to her brother and tried to recall exactly what she had heard. The phone ringing a few seconds after she'd called the pub to say she would be collecting Dad, a slow breathing through the earpiece, and then the voice. The young, appealing voice that time had not altered. Like Peter Pan, Simon Lent could not grow old. Like the Wandering Jew, he could not die. Like the Mad Hatter, he had a fondness for riddles.

'Don't you recognize me, Betty? Aren't you pleased to know that I'm back, the poor little nephew you used to cuddle in the old days?' The words had been interrupted by sobs and giggles, but there was no mistaking the speaker.

A child who had found his parents rotting in a bath. A boy who had hated the house in Sunderland Terrace and experienced hell at Glendale Road School. A man who had posted a suicide note from Australia. A coward who had failed to honour his promise. An evil spirit who had defied death and come home.

'How brave is a coward, Betty? How strong is the soul?' Simon Lent appeared to have read Betty's thoughts through the telephone wires. 'Bill used to be brave, but he's terrified now, and his terror is justified, because I'm strong. Your Billy did see a ghost on the bridge last night, but the ghost has hands and muscles and a brain to control them. I can carry a sack of stones as well as Billy, but I can't ... can't carry my cross any longer.' The voice had faltered before quoting a line from the Bible. ' "Let the dead bury their dead," Betty Smith. Give me peace or I will pull you down into the fire that is burning my life away. You know what you have to do, Betsy, and you're going to do it.' There was another pause, another sob and then a giggle and a snatch of song. ' "Old Macdonald had a farm – Ee-I-Ee-I-Oh." Remember what happened on that farm, Betty. Remember the farmer.' The words stopped and the phone clicked into silence.

'But what have we to do, Betsy?' Billy Smith was standing near the doorway, and he longed to turn the knob and pull the door open. He longed to get out of the room and run. To run away from Betty's repetitions and the faces of his parents and the face in his head. The face of a dead man who kept taunting him. 'We all know that Simon killed himself, so what does he want? Why has his ghost come back to haunt us?'

'You know perfectly well what Simon Lent wants, son, and you'd better use your intelligence for once in a while.' Though Billy had appealed to his sister, it was the mother's voice that answered him. 'You are not a fool, boy, and

Simon is not a ghost. He is very much alive and all he wants from you is money.' Dorothy Smith's words cracked in his ears like pistol shots. 'Simon Lent has a debt to pay and he needs money. A lot of money, though not the kind of money you draw out of your wage packet. Money which you and your sister will have to find, Bill, and I'd advise you to find it quickly.'

The woman was correct and if Simon Lent had been able to hear her he might have nodded approvingly. He was desperate for money and it wasn't the sort of money which would please a banker or a shopkeeper or satisfy a creditor. Simple Simon had no interest in cash, cheques, bearer bonds or dividends. He wanted real money ... red money ... blood money.

Six

'Let's make ourselves comfortable, my dear, and forget about your boss.' A day had passed and Archie Vayne was paying Betty Smith a call at her place of business. 'Solly and I are old pals and if he was here he'd expect you to give me V.I.P. treatment.' The Colonel found the secretary's ante-room rather dreary and he strode towards a door which was fitted with two lamps, one red and one green, and a notice to deter unwelcome visitors. SIR SOLOMON KAHN, K.C.B. (COMPANY CHAIRMAN). DO NOT ENTER UNLESS GREEN SIGNAL IS FLASHING. Neither signal was in operation, but that didn't worry Colonel Archibald Vayne and he turned the door knob confidently. 'I went to school with old Solly and we had some fine times.' Vayne chuckled at the past memories. 'Shoved his head down a lavatory pan once ... plastered his hair with bacon fat ... invented his nickname, Kikey Kahn.

'No harm meant, of course. Just boyish fun and games. I've always been blessed with a sense of humour and Solly took my pranks in good part ...

'At least I hope he did.' Vayne's chuckles faded after he opened the door because the inner office was vast and its décor and furnishings smacked of megalomania. The enormous desk mounted on a dais reminded him of Chaplin's Hitler. The spotlights positioned to shine straight into a visitor's eyes made him think of Gestapo interrogations. The equally enormous painting behind the desk made him regret his boyish fun. Sir Solomon Kahn's image was larger than life and his expression far fiercer.

His body was draped in the robes of a Knight Companion of the Bath, his left arm rested on a globe of the world and his right index finger was pointing at a slogan cribbed from a female novelist whose name Vayne couldn't remember. 'I DON'T ASK FOR *your* BEST ... I DEMAND *the* BEST.'

'Kikey's got on hasn't he, Miss Smith?' The office was on the top storey of a tower block and he crossed to a window and looked at the factory complex spread out beneath him: workshops and laboratories, storehouses and loading bays. Allied Chemical Industrial Developments made everything from lipsticks to plastic cocoons for the protection of laid-up warships and it even had its own railway siding. Vayne watched a string of container trucks being shunted in from the main line. A.C.I.D. was big business and its chairman was obviously a very wealthy and powerful man: not a man to fall foul of.

Had Solly Kahn really accepted the lavatory and bacon fat incidents in good part? Vayne wondered. Did he really find his nickname funny? Had he been amused by those witticisms at the club? 'Been killing any more animals, Kikey? Driven any more nuts right round the bend today?' He hadn't realized that Solly was quite such a big bug and he'd go a bit easy with him in future, because there was no point in making enemies; not rich and dangerous enemies.

But he was sure that Solly hadn't minded his ribbing, and there was no reason why he shouldn't take the fellow's hospitality for granted. Solly was away in the States and he wouldn't miss an odd cigar. The Colonel mounted the dais and opened a box on the desk top. There were plenty more where these came from and the girl wouldn't split on him. Not if she wanted to keep Father-dear-Father happy. He removed a Corona from the box and winked at Betty Smith. 'You ignore my little failings, Miss Smith, and I'll turn a blind eye on yours.' He winked again while he pierced Sir Solomon Kahn's cigar with Sir Solomon's solid gold piercer, but how bloody stupid he thought as he lit it with Sir Solomon's lighter, which was also gold apart from the mechanism. How crazy can humanity become? Because Peter Smith was determined to preserve a proletarian image, his daughter had pandered to his foolishness and was leading a double life. Factory hand – my foot; Betty the benchworker – 'my eye and Betty Martin'. Vayne smiled at the alliteration and considered the confessions which his quarry had stammered out in the anteroom after he'd run her to earth and discovered what she was. Miss Betty Smith had bettered herself and she'd kept quiet about her success to please poor, dear crippled Dad. She had told Dad that she sometimes came home late because she did charitable work helping social drop-outs, but the only person she wanted to help was Number One. She had attended evening classes and studied accountancy, business management and shorthand typing, and her studies were paying off. Elizabeth Smith had an impressive list of diplomas after her name and she was on top of the world. The boss's personal secretary, the boss's trusted assistant and probably the boss's love bird too, judging by the way she'd winced while he had recounted Kahn's humiliations at school. A randy bastard, Solly. Most Yids were randy, and his wife, Rachel, was nothing to write home about. Archie Vayne didn't blame Solly Kahn if he was having it off on the side, as Peter Smith would have phrased it. Smith's daughter might be a phoney, but she was a damned appetizing piece of crackling and he fancied her himself. He might have made a pass at her if he was not so concerned with less attractive things: a mystery to solve, a murderer to find, lives to protect.

Such a lot of lives. The Colonel walked back to the window and watched the trains go by. The semi-fast from Trafalgar Road to Southcliffe, making up time; the boat express slowing at the signals; two suburban locals. Slow trains and fast trains; drab commuter trains and romantic prestige trains like the Channel Belle. Crowded trains and empty trains and horrible special trains crammed with horrible soccer fans. Hooligans who'd be no loss to God or the world, but it was his job to see that they travelled in safety and he loved his job. Protecting lives and property gave him far more power and responsibility than Sir Solomon 'Kikey' Kahn could ever hope for, despite Kikey's money and his factories and his phoney secretary who acted two parts and adopted two accents. The harsh, twanging cockney she'd used in the pub for Dad's benefit. The pleasantly modulated voice that had greeted him when he first entered her office and then became slurred and faltering when she saw who he was. A voice which was faltering again because he had swung round from the window and resumed his questioning.

'How many times do I have to tell you why I burnt that letter, Colonel Vayne? I was in a state of shock and everything Simon wrote was a lie. Simon Lent never intended to kill himself. He's alive and he's come back to torture us. He wants to destroy the whole lot of us and drive us mad.' Betty Smith was also thinking about voices and she glanced through the open door to the telephone on her desk, praying for a call, but dreading what she would hear if the bell rang. The pathetic voice of the boy who ran away ... the threats of the man who'd come home. 'But why is that letter so important, Colonel? Why do you keep on pestering me?'

'I am not pestering you, Miss Smith, but it is my duty to check every piece of evidence and discover the truth.' Vayne ignored the first question to protect himself. He was not going to tell anyone why the letter was important and he hadn't mentioned it to Ted Morcom or the police. Archie Vayne wasn't going to be accused of incompetence.

A bungler who had allowed a girl to burn a vital clue. The link between Simon Lent, who was presumed to have drowned in Sydney Harbour, and Sean Brady who had been murdered on a stretch of waste land near the Crematorium Bridge. Both men were supposed to have written suicide notes and both notes were false, though they had one thing in common. Archibald Vayne wasn't certain, not absolutely certain, but he was pretty sure that both letters had been written by the same hand.

'Now, let's go back to that phone call, Miss Smith. I want you to tell me exactly what Simon said and how he sounded.' Vayne watched the girl's face and similar expressions appeared in his mind's eye. The mother had looked at him with the same air of martyred bewilderment and so had her brother. So had another young man whose name he'd been trying to remember and had just recalled. Turnbull; yes, Corporal Fred Turnbull had looked like that while he made his confession and his appeal. The contemptible admission that he was a homo, a bloomin' *arser*, as they called them in the battalion. The whining request for a transfer because he was being maltreated by his fellow soldiers.

A request which Vayne had turned down with relish. He liked the thought of the contemptible little pervert having a rough time and homosexuality was a crime in the armed forces. He could have sent Turnbull to the glass house, but a better idea occurred to him and he'd pointed at the man's rifle. 'You've got a gun, Corporal, so why not use it? On yourself, of course.'

Excellent advice, though he hadn't expected it would be taken immediately. The sudden report had almost deafened him and Turnbull's blood and brains had spattered his collar and made a thorough mess of his uniform jacket. They could have made a mess of his career too, but fortunately Sergeant-Major Macdougal, who was present during the interview, had covered up for him. Fortunately the medical officer had suspected that Turnbull was a poor insurance risk for some time. Fortunately the Brigadier shared his own views on queers. Most fortunate that Fred Turnbull was an orphan with no relatives to demand a full enquiry. 'Suicide while the balance of his mind was disturbed' had been the official verdict. 'Goodbye to a load of repellent garbage,' was the popular comment.

But, though Betty Smith's expression might resemble the unlamented corporal's, she was certainly not repellent. She was a deuced attractive filly and lust kept interrupting Vayne's thoughts while she tried to answer his questions.

'I can't really explain what Simon sounded like on the phone, Colonel. I recognized his voice, but it kept changing; giggling one moment and sobbing the next, and he spoke in riddles. Threats and sneers and religious allusions. He quoted a line from the Bible and though I don't remember the verse, it was a sort of demand. He said he'd destroy Billy and me unless we did something for him, but he wouldn't tell me what the thing was.' The girl's forehead puckered in concentration. 'I thought that Simon was mad, but maybe I'm the maniac.

'Yes, that could be it, Colonel Vayne. November 1st; the anniversary of Dad's accident, the day Simon Lent ran away and left us, Billy's first day in charge of the 9.15. We were all thinking about Simon that day, so ain't it possible that we imagined things? That Bill didn't see a living soul on the bridge, and his story drove me batty?' A trace of Betty's assumed cockney accent returned. 'Could that phone call 'ave bin an illusion? A voice from my own brain?'

'I think you could do with some Dutch courage, my dear, and I'm sure that our absent friend, Sir Solomon, can provide us with the necessary ingredients.' Vayne sauntered to a cocktail cabinet which was almost as large and vulgar as the absent friend's desk. 'You and your brother are as sane as I am and you've reason to be frightened. I know that Simon Lent is back in England, though I can't tell you how I know.'

Too right he couldn't tell her. The authorities had decided to keep quiet about Brady's murder for a while and he wasn't going to disobey orders till the moment of truth. That happy moment when the conjurer pulled the rabbit out of his hat. When the public would know that a crazed saboteur had been trapped by a public guardian: clever, astute Archibald Hector Vayne.

'I won't have a drink and neither should you, Colonel.' Betty had tried to stop him, but he pushed past her and opened the cupboard. 'Sir Solomon marks his bottles so that he'll know if the levels have fallen and someone has helped himself without permission.'

'I suppose the old Shylock counts his cigars too, but that won't worry me. Not one jot or tittle, as Solly's forebears probably said while smiting the Philistines.' Vayne puffed at his cigar and filled a glass from one of the tell-tale bottles. Filled it to the brim, because Red Hackle is a superb whisky and far too good to adulterate with water.

'Cheers, Miss Smith, but duty comes before pleasure and we must concentrate on Simon.' Vayne drank with relish and then carried the bottle and the glass to the desk and sat down.

'I believe that Simple Simon's grudge started because he was too bright and a man resented his brightness. A stupid, arrogant man who hoped "ter turn ther lad into a decent workin'-class chap, same as Bill and meself".' The Colonel attempted to mimic Peter Smith with scant success. 'Yes, your father's pride set the ball rolling, my dear. He forced Simon to stay at a school where the other children gave him hell, and I wonder what happened when the boy

64

came home in tears and begged to be released from that school.

'Did he get sympathy or a flogging, Betty? Was it Dad's brutality that drove Simon Lent crazy and made him decide to have his revenge? If that's the case I can't say that I really blame Simon.' Vayne spoke with feeling as he considered Smith's insolence in the public house. 'No, I don't blame him, but I have to stop him, and you're going to help me, Betty. You know Simon Lent ran off to sea because he was responsible for derailing your father's locomotive three years ago. That he destroyed the King of the Road and wrecked the Channel Belle. You know that he went really potty when he learned that your father had survived the wreck. You know that he's come back to do some more killing and it's not just Dad he's after now. Simple Simon Lent wants to get the lot of you: father and son – mother and daughter, the whole happy family. Also the thing that concerns me: an express train.

'No, maybe not the daughter. Maybe he's still fond of the little sister who mothered him when he was a child.' Vayne crooked his finger and grinned as the girl walked up the steps towards him. He was certain Betty Smith was lying and there was evidence to support his certainty; the dumb witness – silence. He took another mouthful of Red Hackle and looked around the huge, splurgy office. An operational centre; the war room of a millionaire industrialist with an intercom set and a row of telephones on the desk. But, though the millionaire was in America, the wheels of industry had to keep on churning, so why was business at a standstill? There must be people wanting to leave messages and memoranda for Solly Kahn to study on his return, but he had been alone with Betty Smith for over half-an-hour and there'd been no messages – no memos – no communications at all. The intercom buzzer had not whirred, the telephones had remained silent and not a single harassed executive had knocked on the ante-room door. If Betty had been expecting him she might have told the receptionist and the switchboard operators that she would not be available till he left, but that wasn't so. Miss Elizabeth Smith hadn't expected him because he had arrived without an appointment. She didn't want to answer his questions and she'd be glad if an interruption terminated their interview. Miss Smith had asked the switchboard to keep the telephone lines open for a personal call.

'You're waiting for Simon Lent to ring you again, and it's time to stop the pantomime, Betty.' Vayne's hand shot out and grasped her arm. 'Simon promised to contact you again this morning, and he's been in touch before, hasn't he? Not just last night, but on several occasions and he hasn't *just* returned from Australia. He's been in England for weeks or even months and you know that, Betty. Simon Lent contacted his kind, motherly sister who'd always helped in the past and she helped him again. He said he was a drug addict desperate for a fix and you stole dope from this factory and gave it to him.' Vayne's grip tightened and his certainty increased. Inspector Mason had no idea how the murderer could have obtained enough heroin to kill Sean Brady, but Archie Vayne knew and soon he'd know the whole damned lot. 'You never realized that Lent was a homicidal maniac and you told him that Billy would be in charge of the 9.15. Dad's train, the old Channel Belle to Lythborne, a train he hated because he hated your father.'

'It's not true.' Betty Smith was struggling to pull herself away from him and her whole body trembled with emotion. 'Simon did say that he might phone me again between eleven-thirty and noon this morning.' She glanced at the office clock and saw that the period had elapsed. 'But that was the only time I heard from him and I never gave him a thing. I was sure that Simon Lent was dead till Billy said that he'd seen him on the bridge.

'And he is dead.' She stopped struggling and spoke with the same absolute assurance as her brother had done during his interrogation at the station. 'Simon's body died, but his memory or his spirit has lived on to torment us. Billy and I and our parents are the crazy ones and it's guilt that's driving us crazy. Simon loved us, but we let him down. We left Simon alone at Glendale Road School while those brutes bullied him.

'Brutes rather like yourself, Colonel Vayne, judging from the way you treated Sir Solomon Kahn.' She looked at the portrait of her employer as though hoping that he would step out from the canvas and help her. 'Three brutal bullies made Simon's life a hell on earth and the teachers stood by and did nothing. There was a girl called Kathleen Clarke, a boy called Ray Denton and a man, a sort of man. Sean ... Sean ... I can't remember his surname, but he resembled you, Colonel.'

'Stop being insolent and tell me the truth, Betty.' Vayne pulled her towards him and lifted a heavy ornamental ruler from the desk. His temper was up and he hardly heard her screams or noticed her struggles. He didn't notice the glass and the cigar fall on to the floor to stain and singe Sir Solomon's thick, custom-woven carpet. He just knew that his suspicions were right and the girl was a liar. Simon Lent had returned from Australia and told Betty Smith where he was hiding.

'The truth, girl. I want the truth here and now and I'll knock it out of you if necessary.' She was bent over his knee, the ruler was poised to strike and Vayne would have fulfilled the threat if the door hadn't opened. A powerful man, Archie Vayne; powerful and merciless, but his blow was not delivered. As he himself might have quoted, 'A strong man keepeth his house in order till a stronger cometh', and stronger men had come: two of them.

Betty's cries had sounded the alarm and a pair of dogs had rushed to rescue the chicken from the fox. The leader was blond and wore the uniform of a security guard, and his fellow hound was a Negro chauffeur with a briefcase in his hand. They were both enormous and even if the guard had been in plain clothes and the Negro hadn't lowered the case and drawn a cosh from his jacket pocket, Vayne would have recognized their occupation and temperaments. He had to defend himself from two dedicated professionals. Thugs who not only enjoyed their work but loved it; and he pushed Betty aside and prepared for battle. Though the odds against him were heavy, nobody likes being blinded by jagged glass and there was a weapon handy. Vayne broke the whisky bottle against the edge of the desk and watched the Negro advancing towards him with the cosh dangling and an unpleasant gleam in his bloodshot eyes. He was about to slash at those eyes, when he saw that resistance was useless. The guard was more formidably armed and he appeared to be a reader of American crime fiction. He certainly had an American revolver and it was pointing at Vayne's stomach.

'Put that toy away, Buster, unless you want me to give you a second navel.' He smiled cheerfully when Vayne dropped the bottle and he laughed as his partner flailed out with the cosh. Not a hard blow, just the beginning of the fun. A sharp rap across the Adam's apple that made the Colonel grunt like a broken winded horse and reel back towards Betty Smith. The prelude to the real and richly deserved beating of a rapist. The punishment of a sadistic maniac who had broken into the boss's office and attacked the boss's secretary. Well, the sadist had been caught red-handed and he was going to get a taste of his own medicine. A good time would be had by all.

68

So what was wrong? Why wasn't the maniac whimpering and pleading for mercy? Why wasn't the sadist cowering away from the cosh? The guard's smile faded because their prisoner had started to smile and his grunts had changed to cries of relief. 'Thank Jesus you're here, old boy.

'Oh, sorry for the slip of the tongue. Forgot that you're not a Christian. Thank Moses and Judas and Caiaphas, Kikey, but tell your apes to lay off,' said Archibald Vayne.

Sir Solomon Kahn had returned a week before schedule because his mission to America had flopped and his reception had been horrible. After five days he'd decided that Gehenna was a lesser hell than New York and he'd fled to the airport and boarded the first available flight for London.

He and the company solicitor had gone to the States to try to settle a series of legal claims out of court and they had failed miserably. Though the compensation A.C.I.D. offered was princely in Kahn's opinion, the plaintiffs were represented by hard, grasping lawyers who'd rejected the terms with contempt. Though he knew that the newspapers might be hostile, he had never expected such exaggerated distortions of the truth, and he'd certainly not believed that the television interviewer could treat him so cruelly. Not in all his born days, and the memory had haunted him across every mile of the Atlantic. It would probably continue to haunt him for the rest of his life if the film was shown in England.

After the press conference he had been prepared for more criticism, but the interviewer, Gabriel Winston Meaker, had been kindness itself during the first part of the programme. He had sympathized with Sir Solomon's feelings, agreed that Allied Chemical Industrial Developments' offer was generous and nodded understandingly when Sir Solomon admitted that there had been some slight carelessness in marketing the product. Negligence caused by the urge to sell a hot property, but definitely not criminal negligence; nothing to be really ashamed of.

'I am sure that our audience and all the fair-minded American people appreciate your distress, Sir Solomon,' Mr Meaker had said before the break for commercials. 'In my own view, you are more deserving of pity than the pillory.'

Fair comment, though he had been pilloried. The failure of Terapadorm S, the Sleep Drug, had tormented him for four years. It had cost the company millions already and might beggar them if all the claims were paid in full. He did feel guilty and distressed, though he wasn't personally responsible for what happened. His technical advisers had assured him that the stuff was effective, reliable and safe, and the medical journals were favourably impressed. 'A major breakthrough in the treatment of paranoia, schizophrenia and manic depression' was one appraisement. 'A permanent cure for several diseases of the central nervous system' had been another.

So why should people blame him? He wasn't a chemist or a doctor or a psychiatrist. How could he have known that Terapadorm was too effective, too reliable and that its results really were permanent if the dosage was exceeded by less than half a milligramme? Why had Gabriel Winston Meaker broken his word and put him in the pillory?

'Yes, we do appreciate your distress, Sir Solomon.' Mr Meaker had smiled sympathetically after the programme was resumed, but his sympathy was short-lived and the smile had changed to a scowl as a line of trolleys glided on to the stage. Five hospital trolleys screened by white sheets with a white-faced, dark-eyed man and woman beneath each of them. Gabriel Meaker was a skilled producer and he'd told the make-up department exactly what was wanted – plenty of white grease-paint and plenty of eye-shadow.

'But what about other people's distress, Sir Solomon Kahn? The loving ones and their loved ones who were destroyed by A.C.I.D.'s wonder drug?' Meaker's voice had boomed around the studio and he spread out his arms like a hell-fire preacher proclaiming the Day of Judgment. 'Look at those loving ones, and imagine their sufferings; a mother and a son ... a wife, a husband and a daughter. Look at them carefully, Sir Solomon, and then look at those they have lost.' The first trolley had stopped and Meaker strode from the rostrum and laid a hand on the sheet. 'What happened to the victims of your irresponsible money lust, Solomon Kahn? Do you need to be told?'

There was no need and Kahn had not waited for his torturer to pull back the covering and reveal the thing behind it. He had staggered from his chair and stumbled out of the studio, vomiting when he reached the nearest lavatory, holding a handkerchief against his face while he hurried to the exit, and struggling not to vomit again in the taxi that took him to Kennedy Airport. He'd been so nauseated that he almost forgot to phone the solicitor and say he was leaving and wanted a car waiting for him at Heathrow. A car driven by James Slade: big black Jimmy who'd earned a dozen cups for his skill as a heavyweight boxer and served seven sentences for assault and battery and grievous bodily harm. Ex-pug, ex-convict, but one of the few men Kahn trusted and his faith was justified. Loyal Jimmy had hustled him through the group of British reporters who were gathered outside Customs. Kind, sensitive Jim had realized his distress and comforted him like the devoted retainer he was. 'Don't you give a damn about that Winston Meaker or any other Yankee trash, Boss. You're home in England among decent

English folk like me and nobody'll badger you no more. But if they do ...' Jim had flexed his muscles meaningfully and Kahn had seen them bulge against the uniform jacket.

Good, loyal Jimmy Slade. Sir Solomon had felt slightly less depressed by the time Slade parked the Rolls and escorted him to the lift. Negroes were more loyal and devoted than whites, and they were also physically superior: quicker reactions, keener senses of hearing and sight.

Far quicker, much keener. He hadn't noticed anything amiss when Jimmy pushed past him and bounded down the corridor shouting at Parker, the security guard. He didn't know what was wrong till he had joined them in the office and saw a scene that was both disgusting and enjoyable. Elizabeth Smith was lying on the floor, Parker had drawn his revolver, Jimmy Slade was preparing to settle his score with an acquaintance and deliver another blow with the cosh.

'Tell your apes to lay off, Kikey. We're pals, remember ... Old school chums and I can explain everything.' Slade had stepped back, the acquaintance was grinning, but no explanation could save him, because the evidence told its own tale. Betty Smith pulling herself up from the carpet, a cigar smouldering on the carpet, whisky dribbling from the desk top to the carpet and the desk littered with splintered glass. The acquaintance had broken into his office while Parker's back was turned. The pal had stolen and destroyed his property and attacked his secretary. The old school chum was about to receive a hiding which might ... just might, help him to forget Mr Gabriel Winston Meaker and the things under the trolley sheets.

'Yes, there is a perfectly simple explanation, Kikey. Miss Smith slipped and fell. All quite innocent, so please send Uncle Tom and his mate back to their cabins.' Vayne jerked his thumb at Jimmy Slade. 'On your way,

Rastus. Me and Massa's buddies and we's goin' to have a friendly natter.'

'Buddies, chums, pals!' Sir Solomon literally spat out the words and saliva dribbled from his lower lip. He did not regard Archibald Vayne as a friend and he hadn't enjoyed having his head pushed into a lavatory pan and smeared with grease. He hadn't appreciated the Colonel's boyish humour, and he didn't like his nickname or find the japes in the club funny. 'Driven any more nuts right round the bend, Kikey?' He thoroughly disliked Archibald Vayne and only tolerated him because Rachel and his children had been devoted to the brute's unfortunate wife.

But even Rachel would agree that Vayne had overstepped the mark this time. The whip was in his hand at last and he intended to ply it. 'Save your explanations for the authorities, Colonel,' he said. 'Tell the police and the magistrates why you entered my office, assaulted my secretary and damaged my property. Tell them the lot, if you've any vocal chords left after my boys have finished with you

'Get to work on him, Jimmy, and don't spare the horses.' Kahn watched Slade's cosh swing out again and then gasped because it struck the wrong target. Betty's arm had taken the blow and she was standing in front of Vayne as a shield.

'No ... No ... You must stop it. The Colonel did nothing wrong and he told you the truth.' Betty struggled and screeched while Slade tried to push her aside. 'I offered Colonel Vayne a drink and a cigar because he's a friend of yours, Sir Solomon. A friend of mine, too, though he brought me bad news, and that's how the bottle was broken.' Slade had lowered his blackjack and she picked up the Corona and stubbed it out in an ashtray. 'I fainted, Sir Solomon. I fainted and fell on him.'

Seven

'Maybe the girl fell for me emotionally as well as physically, Ted. Perhaps she lied for the sake of my bonny brown hair.' Though Vayne's Adam's apple still hurt him he grinned at Morcom while weaving his Invicta through the thick South London traffic. The memories of humiliation were fading, but the pleasant images remained. The way Solly Kahn had gasped when Betty Smith threw out her arm to protect him. The reluctance with which Solly's black thug had lowered his cosh. His own air of stern authority as he produced his credentials for Solly's inspection.

'I happen to be a senior superintendent of railway security, Sir Solomon, and I called on your secretary to discuss a matter which is both official and personal. I regret that what I said distressed Miss Smith and caused a fit of giddiness, but I do not regret accepting her hospitality. Common courtesy demanded that she should offer a guest refreshments.

'Do you begrudge me a cigar and small glass of whisky, Sir Solomon?' He took another Corona from the box and sneered the title ostentatiously, because there'd be no more friendly Sollys or Kikeys from now on. 'Does an accidental fall justify a vicious bodily attack, Sir Solomon?' He lit the cigar and pointed it at the uniformed guard who was still clutching his revolver. 'I trust you have a permit to carry a pistol, my man, and I would advise you to put it back in the holster immediately.

'That's better.' He nodded coldly after his order was

obeyed, though he was completely baffled. Betty Smith had not fainted or stumbled. He'd pulled her across his knee and he would have carried out his threat to ply the ruler if Solly's hirelings hadn't arrived on the scene. So why had she wanted to protect him? Why had she lied and supported his story?

There could be several answers, but it wasn't the time or the place to consider them. Women were as unpredictable as April showers and the girl might suddenly decide to change her testimony. If that happened he'd be in trouble again and a dignified retreat was the best policy. Miss Smith could do her explaining later.

'Fetch my hat and coat from the outer office, please.' Vayne watched the Negro chauffeur hurry to the ante-room and then gave Kahn a long, thoughtful stare. 'In view of our former friendship, I may decide not to press charges against you, Sir Solomon, but don't count on that. Assaulting a public official during the execution of his duty is a serious offence and my colleagues could insist that I take legal action.

'Thanks.' The chauffeur had returned and the Colonel stifled a smile as he put on his overcoat, because he had a Parthian shot to deliver. Solly Kahn was the first Jew to be admitted into the El Vagabondo Club. With any luck he'd be the first to be booted out of it. 'I shall naturally have to inform our club committee that you organized an attack on a fellow member, Sir Solomon, but don't let that worry you. You'll be spared the cost of next year's sub-scription.' He had pulled at the cigar and strode away leaving four unhappy people behind him. A girl trying not to sob though the bruise on her elbow was throbbing painfully, and three worried men deprived of pleasure and revenge.

'Yes, Ted, women do find me attractive, but I'm not conceited enough to imagine Betty Smith was motivated

75

by desire.' Vayne lifted a hand from the steering wheel and rubbed the long, white scar which was one of his attractions. *'War wound — Tried to save a chap's life and failed — Sad business — Prefer not to talk about it.'* That explanation always aroused female passion and it was a man's duty to please the ladies. Why admit that he'd fallen down a lavatory staircase when he was tight?

'That girl is concealing something, Ted, and she's also terrified. She wanted to spill the beans and ask me for help, and if those Barbary apes hadn't barged in I'd have conquered her fears and got the truth out of her.

'But not to worry, son. Miss Betty Smith will keep in touch and I'll wager my last farthing that there'll be a message from her waiting for me when we get back to the office.' Vayne saw a gap in the traffic and he stamped on the accelerator and sent the Invicta hurtling forward. A lovely car in his opinion, but Ted Morcom did not share the view and he gripped the door to steady himself as they shot across a road junction missing a bus by inches. A horrible, noisy, boastful car which was as vulgar and loud-mouthed as its owner, and he couldn't imagine why people treasured such monsters and regarded them as collectors' pieces. Morcom had the collecting bug himself, but his tastes were civilized. French carriage clocks, Victorian dolls and other dolls that he showed only to close friends. Japanese figurines of seated women which looked so prim and dainty till one turned them upside down and giggled.

A bit perverse, slightly kinky but quite innocent and no danger to life, limb and property. Not a great snorting Juggernaut in the charge of a megalomaniac who sounded his klaxon horns at every pedestrian crossing. A bully who only thought of himself and enjoyed humiliating other people.

'Of course Miss Smith is frightened, Colonel. Her brother

76

could have been killed the other night and she received a threatening telephone call the following evening.' Vayne had jammed on his brakes at red traffic lights and Morcom tried to relax and consider the girl's behaviour. 'You were about to strike her with a heavy, ebony ruler when Kahn's men arrived, so why did she lie on your behalf? In her situation I'd have let them rough you up and then sent for the police.'

'I'm sure you would, Ted, but I've no interest in your behaviour patterns.' The Colonel smiled sourly. 'I don't know why Betty Smith acted as she did, but I've got a hunch and my hunches usually turn up trumps. Isn't it possible that Miss Smith suffers from divided loyalties and thought it would be safer to talk to me than the rozzers?' The signal had changed to green and he released the clutch and accelerated again. 'Or maybe the lass hoped to put me in her debt, and if that's true she made a bad mistake. Though I'm a fountain of gratitude, I never let personal feelings interfere with duty.

'But whatever Betty's motives may have been she mentioned a man's first name and I've checked that man's career. Before drink and dope sent him to the devil, he worked here, poor sod.'

The Colonel spoke with emotion because their destination was in view. A rambling complex of modern one-storey buildings surrounding the original three-decker block; smoke-blackened brick-barred windows and a general air of Abandon Hope, All Ye Who Enter Here. 'Christ, what a dump!'

'Not exactly an alma mater, sir.' Neither Vayne nor Morcom needed a sign to show that they'd come to the right place, because pictures of Glendale Road School had been displayed on the television and in the newspapers recently. 'Self-discipline or Anarchy' ... 'Education versus Hooliganism', were two of the Press headlines and after

77

Vayne drew up before the main entrance, he saw that the battles had been lost. Anarchy was rampant and hooligans of both sexes surged around the Invicta demonstrating their self-discipline and command of the English language. 'Whatter yer got there, mate?' 'Pinched it outter a museum, eh?' 'Where's ther fuckin' 'orse?'

'Remove your filthy, deformed hands from my bonnet this instant.' Vayne climbed out flushed with fury and also preparing to enjoy himself. One of his happiest commands had been an army detention centre and if he could make grown soldiers squirm, what couldn't he do to children?

'Yes, I'm talking to you, son, and as you appear to be hard of hearing I'll loosen your ears and belt you from hell to Halifax.'

'Yer can't hit me, Mister.' Vayne was glowering at a long-haired youth fingering the radiator badge, but the threats failed and the offender stood to his guns. 'Not 'ere yer can't because Stanny Wolfe, the Community Leader, don't allow no corporal punishment. This is a progressive school with a pupils' union committee runnin' it.'

'And I presume that you are a union official.' Vayne's scowl changed to a friendly grin and he glanced at the Invicta's open exhaust system protruding from the engine cowling. 'I thought so, and please forgive my jokes. Of course I won't hit you. I like chaps who know their rights and you're just the kind of intelligent young man who might help me. I have an appointment with Mr Wolfe and I'd be grateful if you'd keep an eye on my car till I get back.'

'How much is the job worth?' Vayne's smile widened at the question and he jingled the change in his pocket. 'A fair enquiry which deserves a fair answer, and the answer is that I shall pay you in kind.' His arms shot out, but there was no money between the fingers which grasped

78

the boy's wrists and forced his hands down on to the hot silencer pipes.

'Sorry about that. Very clumsy of me but I'm sure you'll understand that it was an unfortunate accident.' Vayne released his grip and addressed the other children, raising his voice to drown the victim's wails of anguish. 'I think we all understand each other and if any lout or loutess touches my vehicle, I won't just scorch the flesh next time. I'll burn you to the bone.

'My colleague will remain in the car and heaven help you if he reports the slightest insolence.' He nodded to Morcom and then reached out again and clutched a smaller and younger boy by the ear. 'And you, my poppet, will now take me to your leader.'

'Yes, Colonel, Sean Brady was employed here as an assistant caretaker, but I can't remember much about him.' Though Stanley Wolfe drew a head teacher's salary, he was not Vayne's idea of a headmaster and he bore no resemblance to his canine namesake, apart from a set of large, loose National Health dentures. He couldn't even rank as a wolf in sheep's clothing. He was just a dim-witted sheep as Vayne had suspected from the newspaper reports, and his suspicions had been verified before he reached the man's office. The noisy, disorganized class-rooms and the corridors thronged with clamouring morons and smirking adolescent whores had told him a great deal about Community Leader Wolfe, as the fool called him-self. Stanley Wolfe preached free-discipline because he was unable to enforce discipline. He had abolished normal teaching methods because he and his staff lacked the ability to teach. He was a contemptible hypocrite and a most unhelpful person.

'The Smiths ... William and Elizabeth.' Wolfe had opened a file and shrugged his sloping shoulders. 'I do recall them and, as this record shows, they were a difficult couple. The boy had five "O" levels and two "A" levels, and the girl was offered an art scholarship. What you and I would have called swots in our younger days, Colonel, and not at all the kind of material Glendale Road usually turns out.' Mr Wolfe frowned sadly and clicked his false teeth.

'We don't believe in formal instruction or academic distinctions here, Colonel Vayne. Children are not computers to be programmed and controlled. Units for pedants to categorize as the élite and the deprived. Each child in our charge is equal in the Creator's sight and must express himself freely, though as a member of the group.

'I use the word Creator loosely, of course, as any rational agnostic may.' He paused because one of his charges had just expressed its freedom and the door shuddered under the impact of a football.

'But the Smith children lacked the communal spirit and kept themselves to themselves. An over-close and unhealthy relationship based on snobbery which the parents encouraged despite my disapproval. Billy and Betty Smith imagined they were superior to their fellow team-mates and that is a very objectionable thing in my view.

'A view which I'm sure you share, Colonel.' He nodded at Vayne's old Harrovian tie. 'After all, the public schools were our first true comprehensives.'

'Afraid I'm not an educationalist, Mr Wolfe, though ... ' Vayne had been about to say that, judging from what he'd seen of the team-mates, it would be difficult not to develop a superiority complex, but a second thud of the football gave him time to think again. Mr Stanley Wolfe was a despicable sheep, but he needed the sheep's co-operation. He had to find a murderous train-wrecker, and motivation might lead him to his quarry. A crazy vendetta that had started at Glendale Road three years ago and Betty Smith had mentioned three people. A girl called Kathleen

Clarke, a boy called Ray Denton and a man … 'a sort of man', whose surname Betty had forgotten. Sean Joseph Brady with his torn body lying in a morgue freezer.

'We're all entitled to our personal opinions, Headmaster, but as you know I'm conducting an official enquiry, and several of your former pupils may be involved in the business. So, what can you tell me about the Smiths' nephew, a boy named Simon Lent?'

'Lent … Lent … Simon Lent.' Wolfe repeated the name slowly and Vayne noticed some very interesting things. Mr Stanley Wolfe hadn't liked the question. The repetition was an attempt to give himself time to think, and his eyes were frightened. The stupid, panic-stricken eyes of a stupid cowardly man with a secret to hide. Community Leader Wolfe was troubled by a guilty conscience.

Significant signs of deceit and emotion, but another thing Vayne had seen was the most interesting of all. He had a friend at court, an ally to rely on.

'Yes, Lent, sir, and you don't need a file to refresh your memory.' Wolfe was opening a drawer, but the Colonel leaned forward and banged his fist on the desk. 'You know who I'm referring to, so stop stalling and tell me the truth. What did your free-expressionist band of illiterates do to Simon Lent, Headmaster?'

'I honestly do not know, Colonel, and please stop calling me *headmaster*. The title is a relic of feudalism like Squire or Matron and I much prefer Community Leader.'

'I prefer the title Prevaricator, Mr Wolfe, and you are still stalling.' Vayne's fist thumped the desk even more loudly. 'You and your staff must have realized Simon was having a rough ride and I want to hear who was responsible.'

'How can I tell you something I don't know myself, Colonel, and only a couple of my present staff were here at the time.' Wolfe cowered in his chair as though fearing that Vayne's next blow would be directed at him person-ally. 'Liberal education has its trials as well as rewards, and many teachers can't stand the pace. They ask for transfers or complain of nervous breakdowns. They desert me like troops fleeing from a battle.

'As a soldier you will understand that, Colonel.' He appealed for sympathy but it was not forthcoming. If any soldier had deserted Archie Vayne during a battle, he'd have shot him on the spot or ordered a court martial. 'I couldn't prevent the children resenting Simon. The boy invited antagonism, and he couldn't accept horseplay in good part. If you can remember your own schooldays you must agree that a bit of rough and tumble is a com-mon phenomenon and sometimes impossible to detect till the victim cracks. You must know how cruel youngsters can be to an individual who provokes them.'

'Of course I know, Mr Wolfe.' A fleeting memory of Solomon Kahn's head suspended over the lavatory crossed Vayne's mind, but there were other memories which were just as pleasurable and he stared at a notice board behind Wolfe's desk. A list of the school departments followed by the teachers' names, qualifications and length of service.

Memories and coincidences, and there were a lot of the latter. Strange that Pam should have died so conveniently on the 9.15. Strange that he was investigating a second attack on the train that killed her. Strange that Betty Smith should be employed by Kikey Kahn, his former buddy. Strangest of all was an entry on the board and it made him think that pure chance could not explain the sequence of events. He was the hero of a Greek play, con-trolled by destiny and the gods, and they were on his side. Nemesis had ordained Pam's death. Fate had laid a guiding hand on his shoulder and the wheels of fate were bearing him on to glory. The wheels of the Channel Belle which would roll on till he found the wrecker. Fate had provided him with a staunch ally and while he looked at the list Vayne nearly burst into song.

> 'Oh, I've got a friend beside me,
> To guide me ... always.'

'DEBATES & DISCUSSIONS – Isabel Pounder, B.A. (One Term).'
'DRAMA & DANCING – John Thompson, R.A.D.A.; Johnny Thomas to you, lassies. (One term and three months.)'
'CREATIVE EXPRESSION – Cynthia ... "Sinny" Mossop, Dip. Ed. (Five weeks).'

As Wolfe had admitted, his troops soon fled the field and most of the appointments were recent and would probably be short-lived. The holders would move off to quieter establishments or mental wards, but two stalwarts had stood their ground and Vayne knew one of those stalwarts. He knew him and respected him almost as highly as he respected himself, and the very name told him that fate was guiding him. Coincidences happen daily, but fortune had given him a trusty ally, a survivor who had never run from a battlefield. A hero who'd survived Alamein and D-Day and the Rhine Crossing. Who had come through Korea and was a friend in past deed and present need. A friend whose title and honours were proudly displayed on the board, and no juvenile delinquents had cut short his length of office.

'DEPARTMENT OF WOODWORK, METALWORK AND PRACTICAL ENGINEERING – Regimental Sergeant-Major Donald Macdougal, V.C., M.M. (Seven years).'

Eight

'Grand to see you again, Colonel surr. Always a pleasure to welcome an old comrade-in-arms.' Regimental Sergeant-Major Macdougal had a whistling Scottish accent and apart from his voice and a hum of ordered activity the workshop was silent. The whole science department seemed a haven of silence compared to the clattering main building and Vayne felt as though he had walked out of a zoo monkey-house into the peace of an aquarium. 'How long is it since we last served together, surr? Must be fifteen years or more, but you don't look a day older. I recognized you the moment that loon Wolfe opened the door and interrupted me wee nap.'

'You haven't aged either, R.S.M.' Vayne was staring at his former comrade with something akin to awe. He'd always known that Donald Macdougal was a stern disciplinarian, but he appeared to be a miracle-worker too. The 'wee nap' had been a deep sleep and he was dead to the world before Wolfe disturbed him. His squat, craggy body slumped comfortably in a chair, his feet were propped up on a desk and snores ruffled his gingery moustache.

'Teaching obviously agrees with you, but how the hell do you do it?' Vayne turned and studied the class. Fifty boys and girls of the same moronic types that had surrounded his car and jostled him in the corridors and kicked a football against Wolfe's door. But all docile and organized and industrious. All intent on their tasks. The boys working busily away with drills and pliers, screwdrivers and soldering irons. The girls operating typewriters, knitting needles and sewing machines.

'Aye, I enjoy me job, Colonel. Always fancied meself as a schoolmaster, and I went to a training college after leavin' the service. Not that I got any training. The lecturers were all as wet as Stan Wolfe, and yer can't be much wetter than him.' Macdougal grimaced in disgust and then suddenly clapped his hands together. Not a loud clap, but every member of the class stopped work and stared up at him.

'What are you doing, David Nolan? Do you want to beggar us, or have you forgotten that thrift is a virtue?' He questioned a boy who was holding a soldering iron over a radio chassis. 'Don't you know the current price of lead?

'Aye, thirteen pounds a hundredweight, so go easy with it, lad, and smear the contacts lightly.' The Sergeant-Major spoke more in sorrow than anger. 'You're assembling transistors, Davie, not welding a ruddy battleship.

'Right, you can all get on with your tasks and please remember that we're working on miserly profit margins.' He watched his pupils resume activity and sighed at Vayne. 'A good bunch, sir, but wasteful like most bairns. Terribly extravagant and wanton with materials.'

'But how do you control them, Mr Macdougal?' Vayne was still studying the good bunch whose faces seemed to vary from sly cunning to brutish stupidity. 'How did you manage to teach them anything?'

'Discipline is no problem, surr. They control themselves because they're paid by results. Isn't that correct, Eileen Kirby?' He addressed a girl sitting at a sewing machine, but she was too busy to answer verbally and merely nodded. 'Aye, by results, lassie, and you've got six more skirts to hem before the end of the period.

'As for teaching the brats anything, Colonel,' Macdougal

lowered his voice slightly, 'I only discovered one useful thing at that training college, but it stood me in good stead. Our educational system is a flop because eighty per cent of the so-called students don't want to be educated, and no sane person can blame them. Would you want to sit through an algebra lesson if you weren't even capable of filling in a football coupon? Would you enjoy Miss Cynthia Mossop's Creative Expression Groups, if you were tongue-tied?

'Of course you wouldn't, surr, and neither would I. We'd give Sinny Mossop merry hell as this gang will be doing in an hour.

'In less than an hour, Chundra Lal, and those cigarette lighters must be ready then.' Macdonald's next target was an Indian boy who had paused to blow his nose. 'Ready and checked because Mr Lazarus insisted on a penalty clause for late delivery and the contract expires today.

'However, though these bairns are slow-witted, Colonel, they can master simple, mechanical skills and many small firms are prepared to pay for their skills. You'd be surprised how many, and that's why we are such a contented gathering. There's nought wrong with honest toil and the labourer is worthy of his hire.

'Eileen Kirby, whom I just spoke to, hasn't an ounce of creative talent and she's far happier hemming skirts for money than slapping paint and clay around the art room. Joshua N'Gomo over there is too shy to speak English, so what good are Miss Pounder's Debates and Discussions to him?' He pointed at a Negro boy fiddling with the blade of a hacksaw and frowned. 'Joshua, son, how often must I tell you that teeth have to face downwards. Smooth edge not cut 'em? ... Sharp side make clean chop-chop.

'No, surr, education without incentive is bound to fail whether it's formal or free, but my system works wonders. The firms are happy because I can quote low tenders. The kids are happy because I pay 'em half the profits. The inspectors are happy because this is the only department in the menagerie where they know they won't get a boot or a cricket ball slung at them. The school managers are happy because we cause no trouble and they've told Stanny Wolfe to leave us alone. One or two of 'em even benefit from our operations and Isaac Lazarus is chairman of the board.'

'And you must be happy with the other half-share of the profits, R.S.M.' Though Vayne's admiration was still rising, it was tempered by envy and he almost wished he'd taken up teaching himself. 'Tax-free profits and quite a tidy little sum I imagine.'

'Not bad, Colonel, but peanuts to what that selfish bitch gets.' Macdougal motioned Vayne towards a glass partition revealing another room and another group of industrious toilers. A smaller group, but of higher quality than the R.S.M.'s. Technicians were checking mathematical data, examining engineering drawings for stress and strain, and performing other complicated operations which Vayne couldn't fathom. Presiding over them was another sleeper, an obscenely fat woman with her mouth open and breasts heaving in peaceful repose.

'That's my oldest colleague, Molly Lardner, Colonel, though there's little love between us. Because Molly has a science degree she grabs the cream and her kids work for accountants, architects and so forth. They earn twice as much as mine and it's no' fair.' He stood up and eyed his recumbent colleague with loathing. 'When I suggested we should go into partnership and split the proceeds fifty-fifty, the mean-minded slave-driver laughed at me. Swollen with money as well as flesh is Molly Lardner.

'But I'm sure you didn't come here to talk about education or Mrs Lardner, Colonel Vayne, so how can I oblige you?' He turned from the partition and raised his eyebrows. 'Are you in business yourself, perhaps? Do you need a bit of work done on the side?'

'I'm in business, Sergeant-Major, but it's governmental business and what I need is information.' Vayne produced his credentials. 'I want you to cast your mind back three years and tell me what you know about five people. A brother and sister named Smith, a boy and a girl called Ray Denton and Kathleen Clarke, a caretaker whose name was Sean Brady, a third boy ... '

'Simon Lent.' Macdougal interrupted him with a low, urgent whisper. 'Why the hell can't you leave well alone, surr? Three years is a long time, so why dig up the past? The polis were satisfied that it was an accident. A nasty affair, but only an accident; nothing of a criminal nature.

'Och, verra well, I'll tell you what I know, but not here. We'll pop along to me den and have a quiet chat.' He moved to the door and then clapped his hands again. 'Me and this gentleman have private business to discuss, boys and girls, and I'm relying on you to behave yourselves during my absence. There must be no idling, no sloppy work and no sinful waste of materials.' Macdougal paused and delivered his final plea mournfully. 'Above all remember that a contract's a contract and we can't afford to pay penalties for late delivery. Whatever happens, Mr Lazarus mustn't be kept waiting.'

'You believe that Simon Lent really has come back, Colonel? That Billy Smith actually did see him on that bridge and it was his voice Betty heard on the phone? That Lent wrote the suicide note they found in Sean Brady's pocket?' Macdougal had ushered Vayne into his den. A room which was both Spartan and comfortable and as near to a military office as he could make it. Time-tables, work rosters and group photographs of soldiers and schoolchildren lined the walls, sporting trophies gleamed on shelves, and two highlights of his career were proudly displayed above the fireplace flanked by an Italian helmet and a Nazi dagger. Blown-up snapshots of himself shaking hands with Churchill and being patted on the shoulder by Field Marshal Montgomery.

'Aye, it's possible I suppose, Colonel. I can credit anything I hear about young Lent. Sabotage, blackmail, murder; Simon Lent was capable of the lot.' He motioned Vayne to an armchair, but remained standing. 'That lad was a nutter all right and he might enjoy smashing trains. But three years is a longish time and I can't see how I can help you find him. No specimens of his writing will be on record now, and I don't remember whether he was left-handed.'

'I'm more interested in Lent's mind and motives than his handwriting and I think the motivation started here, Donald.' Since they were alone Vayne had discarded formality, though he'd have been furious if Macdougal had followed suit and called him Archie. 'I think Simon Lent dreamed up a vendetta because of something which happened in this school, and you're probably the only teacher who knew the boy personally.

'What did happen, Donnie? What drove Lent round the bend and made him a nutter, as you put it? Did ordinary bullying, horseplay, and a bit of rough and tumble send Simon Lent running off to sea?'

'Horseplay ... Rough and tumble? Those phrases sound like Stanley Wolfe, surr.' Macdougal smiled, but there was no humour in his face and no sneer or cynicism either. He just moved his lips and his eye muscles and the gesture meant nothing at all. 'Ordinary bullying ... horseplay?

'Well, I suppose one shouldn't blame Stanny Wolfe for protecting himself and it wasn't really his fault.' He opened a tobacco pouch and fumbled with a charred briar pipe. 'We've got over a thousand kids in this school

89

and Stan probably didn't notice what was going on. Thinks of himself more as an admin type than a teacher, though he's not fit to run a public lavatory.'

'But you knew what was going on, Donnie.' Vayne watched the man preparing his pipe with infinite slowness; blowing down the stem, knocking out the ash and sniffing the tobacco before rolling it between his fingers. Like Stanley Wolfe, Regimental Sergeant-Major Donald Macdougal wanted time to think because he had something to hide ... something discreditable.

'Stop dithering, Donnie, and tell me about Lent.' Vayne pointed at one of the military photographs and saw three familiar faces staring back at him. His own face, Macdougal's face and the face of a dead homosexual. 'We're old friends and comrades, Donnie, and we can trust each other. You covered up for me after Corporal Turnbull shot himself, and I'll do the same for you. If you did anything that might cost you your job or your pension, I won't breathe a word about it.'

'You believe that I'm worried about the job, Colonel?' At long last the pipe was ready and as Macdougal struck a match and held it over the bowl, the flare lit up his eyes and revealed a truth which Vayne had never thought possible. Donald Macdougal had been awarded the Victoria Cross and a Military Medal for conspicuous gallantry. Vayne had personally witnessed him storm a machine-gun post single-handed during a retreat, and imagined the man was incapable of fear.

But he was wrong, and Macdougal was not merely worried and furtive as Stanley Wolfe had been. He was terrified, and after the pipe was alight, his teeth clenched the mouthpiece as wounded soldiers once bit on bullets to stifle pain.

'Och, to hell with me job, surr, and to hell with me pension too. I've no family to support and I can manage on what I get from the army. I've also saved a bit out of those bairns' earnings.' A trace of his former brashness returned, but only briefly and he removed the pipe from his mouth and frowned at a calendar.

'Guy Fawkes Night tomorrow, Colonel. The fifth day of November; the day of the fires. The fifth day after Hallowe'en when Satan releases the damned from hell.

'Do you believe in Satan, surr? Do you believe in hell fire and eternal damnation? Is it possible that a tortured soul may be granted a spell of freedom? That an evil spirit can return from the grave to harry us?'

'I believe in facts, Mr Macdougal, and one fact is obvious.' The man was becoming incoherent and Vayne's informality stopped abruptly. 'You are concealing evidence from me and I am a British Rail Superintendent investigating a case of murder and attempted sabotage.' He stood up and also drew himself up, because he'd been trained to handle soldiers and knew how to open a military mind. 'I was also your commanding officer, so come to your senses and answer my questions.' He straightened his spine like a ramrod, squared his shoulders and bellowed an order. 'Ten-shun, Sarn't-Major.

'That's better.' Conditioning had worked and Macdougal reacted like a machine. The pipe dropped from his hand, his heels clicked together and his own spine stiffened. 'Much better, R.S.M., and I am now ready to hear your report on Private Simon Lent.'

'Missin' and presumed dead, Colonel. Deserted after a charge of insubordination. Left camp and ran away.' The voice was the voice of an automaton and only the eyes showed human emotion. 'Lent's loss was discovered on November 2nd and six other persons may be involved. Train driver Peter Smith. Boy and girl, named Ray Denton and Kathleen Clarke. A caretaker, Sean Brady.

'Also a second boy: William Smith, son of the first

victim. Lucky escape there, surr ... Most fortunate ... Providential, one might say, but what about Number Six?' Ingrained discipline had acted as potently as a drug, but its effects were brief. Macdougal's body relaxed and he stooped to retrieve his pipe.

'Aye, what about Number Six, Mr Safety Superintendent Vayne? Can you and providence protect old Donnie Macdougal?'

Nine

Trains roared and clattered under the bridge, and cars and lorries rumbled above it. Children were shouting on a football field and an ambulance siren wailed in the distance. Organ music drifted from the chapel and a priest was intoning the Nunc Dimittis beside a grave. There was little wind and the air smelled of flowers and exhaust fumes and a faint tang of smoke from the crematorium chimney. Footsteps crunched on gravel as a boy and a girl walked between the dead.

'Can't you understand that I had to protect Vayne, Billy? Don't you realize what would have happened if Kahn had let those men rough him up and then sent for the police?' Betty Smith gripped her brother's hand tightly. 'Vayne is a blustering bully but no fool, and he'd have a story ready to tell the magistrates. He could have said that I was a hysterical nymphomaniac, a masochist who had asked him to beat and rape me.'

'And they might have believed the bastard.' Bill watched a hearse and three black limousines moving slowly towards the chapel. Business was brisk today and as soon as one funeral procession left another drove in. 'Yes, they might have believed him, because it would be your word against his and Colonel Archibald Hector Vayne's an honourable, distinguished gentleman with a Military Cross to his credit and bags of phoney charm. In any event the police would have checked your character and you'd be in trouble, Betty. How would Dad have reacted after a detective called at the house and told him the truth?

'So that's it, lass. That's what yer' are, Betsy.' Billy reproduced his father's accent savagely. 'No honest working lass on factory floor, but a bleedin', lyin', stuck-up Madam. The boss's secretary ... Solomon Kahn's little lap-dog bitch.' Not only the voice was reproduced. Billy's left arm dangled loosely from the shoulder as though it was paralysed and his feet shuffled the gravel chippings. 'Well, Madam's lies 'ave bin found out, 'aven't they, and the lap-dog's due for a taste of me belt. I'm goin' to flog her like I flogged our Billy, lass.'

'Stop it, Bill. Stop mocking a poor helpless cripple who can't flog anybody. Dad's hardly able to unbuckle his belt now and that crash broke his spirit as well as his body.' Betty glanced back at the railway bridge. 'I wasn't frightened *of* Dad but I'm frightened *for* him. I'm frightened for the lot of us, darling; for you and me and Dad and Mum. This nightmare has got to end before it destroys us.'

'You mean, before *he* destroys us, Betty.' The boy's arm stiffened, the limp vanished and he spoke normally, though with a trace of bewilderment. 'But maybe he can't hurt us and it is just a nightmare; a bad dream that will pass in time.' They had reached the older section of the cemetery and Billy studied the rows of pretentious memorials as though each bronze urn, granite cross and marble angel might be screening a watcher. 'A dream that started up here, because I was worried stiff when they ordered me to take out the 9.15.' He pulled his hand away from hers and tapped his forehead. 'Yes, that could account for everything, because I'm superstitious by nature and I don't like coincidences. The same date, the same train and the same clear evening. That huge yellow moon glittering on the rails and the signals like green stars ... like the eyes of the roundabout horses we rode on when we was kids.

94

'I hated those signals, Betty. I prayed for them to change to red or amber and give me an excuse to stop or slow down. I hated Dick Andrews for telling me to get cracking.' He halted and lowered a haversack on to the path. 'I hated the very feel of the throttle lever till I did what Dick wanted and swung it over to full power.

'But once the power came on and the locomotive started to speed up, I stopped being worried and my brain seemed to accelerate with her. I loved the sound of those pounding diesels and screaming electric motors. I wanted to sing in tune to them like Dad used to do. And after a while I began to imagine that I was Dad. Peter Smith, the King of the Road, roaring down to the coast with the evening Belle behind him.

'Doesn't that explain everything, Betty? If I was reliving the start of Dad's last journey, why not the end? Isn't it possible that Simon Lent is just a dream figure and there was no one on the bridge, no one at all?'

'We've discussed that possibility several times, Bill, and we both know that it's a comforting lie and the truth has to be faced. You did see Simon Lent and I did hear him. We're not insane yet, darling, but Simon will drive us insane unless we get to him first.' It was the girl's turn to stare around the graveyard. 'Simon Lent is alive and he's watching us now. We can't see him at the moment, but he can see us and he can read our thoughts. He can see us and smell us and I think he intends to kill us. I think that he will kill us if we don't lay his ghost or trap his body. The police can't stop Simon, but you and I should be able to, Billy.

'No, not *should* be. We must stop him because Simple Simon is a wounded animal who crawled into a hole to die, and came back to life. Simon can't help his craving for revenge any more than a leech craves for blood, and I don't blame him for what he did and intends to do.

95

'But I'm going to trap him, so let's hope that he'll find the bait tempting; meat to attract a werewolf.' Betty smiled as her brother picked up the haversack and they moved on. On along the gravel paths ... on past the old Victorian monuments ... on towards the far end of the cemetery and humbler memorials marking the cremated dead ... On to a simple slab of grey stone with a simple inscription carved on its weather-worn surface. *'Raymond Denton — born November 5th, 1957 — died on his seventeenth birthday; resting in the Arms of Jesus.'*

'That's a lie, Simon Lent.' Betty Smith raised her voice as her brother opened the bag and pulled out a hammer. 'You thought you killed Ray, but you're wrong and Raymond Denton is not resting with Jesus.' Her voice grew louder and louder and she laughed when the hammer shot home and the slab splintered. 'Ray is waiting for you, Simon, and he'll never rest till you come back and fetch him.'

'I can't tell you whether Simon Lent might have wrecked Peter Smith's train, Colonel, but I do know this.' Donald Macdougal had opened two Guinness bottles and sat down facing Vayne. 'Simon had little reason to love his adopted father and I doubt whether he ever loved a living soul.

'No, maybe that's unfair. The lad probably loved his own parents and the shock of their suicide soured him. Certainly the punishment he got here would have driven a saint over to Satan, but Peter Smith refused to transfer him to another school. If Glendale Road was good enough for his own family, it was good enough for Simon Lent and a bit of rough treatment might make a man of him.

'Your very best health, surr.' Macdougal raised his mug ceremoniously. 'Here's to the fine times we've had together.'

'Cheers, Donnie.' Vayne eyed his host while he swallowed a mouthful of stout. Before opening the bottles, Macdougal had seemed to be on the verge of a nervous breakdown but now his manner was quite normal again and his hand as steady as a rock. 'But Smith told me that he and his son waylaid two boys who had been bullying Simon and the ill-treatment stopped.'

'Did Smith believe that, surr?' The R.S.M. snorted over his glass and a fleck of foam spattered Vayne's jacket. 'I knew the lads well and they told me about it; two brothers called Owen. They had a drubbing all right but that didn't help Simon Lent, because it was their last term. One's a policeman up in Glasgow and the other joined the army and got killed in Ulster.

'Have I said something to upset you, Colonel?' He had noticed Vayne's sudden frown. 'Are you feeling chilly perhaps?'

'It is rather cold, but I'm quite all right.' The frown was due to frustration, because Vayne's theory that revenge for a beating might have led to sabotage had fallen flat. 'The ill-treatment was resumed?'

'It never stopped, surr, and it had started from the moment Simon Lent entered this school, because practically every kid in the place had it in for him.' Macdougal leaned forward and turned on a gas fire in the grate. 'Ill-treatment indeed … horseplay, as Stan Wolfe said. Not a week passed without something happening to Lent. Accidents at first, because Billy and Betty Smith tried to stick up for him, but repetitive accidents. Simon Lent was always the one who got kicked on the football field or jostled down the stairs. It was always Simon who happened to catch his fingers when a door was closing or have a desk top slammed on 'em.

'Aye, he had a hard time with Billy and Betty to protect him, but after they left he must have gone through hell.

97

Even that drunken Irish caretaker, Sean Brady, had a go at the boy. He told Ray Denton and Kate Clarke to drag him down to the furnace room and they roasted his arse against the bars.

'Why didn't the staff stop the bullying, Colonel?' Macdougal seemed surprised by the question. 'How could they when most of them were incapable of running a rabbit hutch? You've seen a few of our classes, so do you think you'd be able to control the whole school?'

'I'm damn certain that I could, Donald.' Vayne thought of another roasting by hot metal and how another boy had yelped and cringed while his hands were forced against an exhaust pipe. 'And so could you, Regimental Sergeant-Major Macdougal. You've no disciplinary troubles, so why didn't you do something for Lent and order the louts to lay off him?'

'Why didn't you order the men in "B" Company to lay off Corporal Turnbull, surr?' Macdougal puffed at his pipe and grinned. 'We're two of a kind you and I, Colonel Vayne, and we've got a lot on our consciences. Turnbull died because you wanted him to die, and Simon Lent ran away because of me. That's why I got nervy when you told me he was back, surr. Why I'm scared out of me wits, and I'll remain scared till we get him.

'I mean *we*, surr, and to hell with the polis. If Simon Lent is alive, you and I are going to take care of him personally because, like I said, we're two of a kind, and dog don't eat dog. We've also got reputations to preserve and that's why I can confide in you, Colonel. If you breathe a word of what I tell you, I'll spill the beans about Fred Turnbull.

'You see it's not fear for me life that's worrying me, surr. The Jerries and the Wops and the Korean Commies couldn't kill Donnie Macdougal, and I'm pretty sure that a nutter like Lent will be equally unsuccessful.' He jerked back his chair and walked over to a cupboard. 'I'm worried about my good name and my liberty, Colonel, and young Lent could rob me of both.

'Young Lent or old Lent? I don't know how old his soul was, because age is relative and I seem to think that it wasn't a boy, but an old-old man who came into my office that day.' There was a window beside the cupboard and Macdougal stared through the glass. First at the playground where a group of children were clumsily building a bonfire in preparation for the next day's Guy Fawkes party. Then at the trains shooting up and down towards the bridge and the railway embankment. Finally at the cemetery and the crematorium; lawns and cypress trees and memorials gay under a bright November sun.

'I tried to fathom Simon Lent when he first arrived here, Colonel, though I'll admit that I didn't try too hard. There was something about him that repelled me. Can't explain it; the sort of revulsion people get from rats and snakes and spiders, but that lad gave me the creeps. I pretended that it was a rational dislike caused by inferiority. By his accent and his background and his intelligence.' Macdougal opened the cupboard and shrugged. 'Simon Lent did make me feel inferior, Colonel, and I wasn't the only one. The little bastard had a genius I.Q. and he could run rings round the lot of us, teachers and kids alike.

'I thought it was simply jealousy that made me keep my mouth shut and let them persecute Simon. Why I didn't tell Ray and Kate to leave him alone ... Why I didn't report Brady to the managers and see that the sod got his marching orders.

'Simon Lent fooled me, surr.' He nodded through the window while opening the cupboard. 'I hadn't a clue what I was up against, but they knew. Youngsters are more intuitive than adults and those blighters could recog-

99

nize a damned soul. An evil spirit that should never have been born.

'But before I get into the confessional box, I'd like to test your religious knowledge, surr. Do you know what is the most stupid verse in the New Testament?' He took a Bible out of the cupboard, and flicked through the pages when Vayne shook his head. 'You disappoint me, Colonel. I always imagined you were a well-educated man, but not to worry. I only spotted the lie myself when that monster with his boy's face and age-old evil came grinning into this office three years ago.' Macdougal had found the passage he wanted and read aloud. 'St John's Gospel, Chapter 15, Verse 25. "They hated me without cause." '

Sergeant-Major Donald Macdougal was right in saying that Simon Lent attracted hatred, but two people had ceased to dislike him. Ray Denton's ashes were buried under a cracked stone slab, and Kathleen Clarke couldn't hate anybody. She couldn't hear anybody or feel anybody or see anybody. All she could see was the ceiling above her and she stared at the white plaster and grinned.

Ten

'Forgive me if I ramble a bit, Colonel, but three years is a long while and I'm trying to push my mind back.' Macdougal had finished his Guinness and he lowered the mug on to the window-ledge. 'Ray Denton had been drinking before the accident, of course. The doctors found 120 milligrammes of alcohol in his blood, and after the police questioned Sean Brady he admitted that he'd given the boy drink. Ray died, Brady got the sack and a year's suspended sentence, but what did my bonnie Kate Clarke get?

'A broken spine and a face to make yer shudder.' Macdougal closed his eyes and pictured the scene. A big Honda motorcycle charging down the motorway with a crazed boy bent over the handlebars and a girl behind him. Had Kathleen been frightened or elated when Ray decided to do a ton? he wondered. Had she screamed when the wheels skidded on the damp tarmac? Had she felt pain before the bike hit the side of a lorry and the lights went out? Questions which would never be answered. Vegetables can't speak and Kathleen Clarke was a cabbage.

'Aye, the coroner said that booze made Ray lose control, surr. He was quite sure that Kate's brain cells withered because the kiss of life had been administered too late, and I accepted his verdict at the time; fool he ... bigger fool, I. Brady's cheap wine didn't send young Denton haywire, and lack of circulation was not the only thing that rotted Kate's brain.' Macdougal watched the children stacking timbers on the bonfire pile and grimaced. 'As I said, kids are more intuitive than us adults, sir, and they gave Simon Lent hell, because they sensed what he was. A creature from hell who drove my lassie to hell ... who murdered Ray Denton as surely as if he'd pumped a bullet through his skull.

'I don't suppose you're partial to sweets, Colonel; toffees and chocolates and suchlike. But Ray and Kate were and they used to help themselves to Simon Lent's goodies. How happy Simon must have been when they pinched his packet of caramel creams.

'Aye, caramel creams with another substance injected into 'em. I canna remember what the stuff's called, but it was made by the firm Betty Smith works for and taken off the market like Thalidomide. Similar name to Thalidomide and equally dangerous, though the effects were different; worse if anything.'

'The name is Terapadorm S, Sergeant-Major, and the effects are common knowledge. But will you please come to the point?' Vayne remembered his jokes in the club. 'Been killing any more animals, Kikey? Driven any more nuts right round the bend today?' The witticisms and Solomon Kahn's embarrassment had seemed funny at the time, but they no longer amused him and he felt slightly sick.

'You may be right, Donnie, but why didn't you tell the coroner what you're telling me? Why have you kept your suspicions to yourself? Though you couldn't have had any proof, it was your duty to make a public statement.'

'I had proof, surr, ample proof.' Macdougal reached into the cupboard again. 'I know exactly what happened, because I heard the murderer's confession, but like yourself I'm blessed with a strong survival instinct.

'I had to keep quiet and this will show you why.' He lifted a metal deed-box from a shelf and more pictures filtered through his mind's eye while he explained his predicament to Archie Vayne.

Shadowy pictures, and he couldn't remember whether he had been angry or surprised at first. There was a notice outside his study door which no pupil had ever disregarded. KNOCK BEFORE ENTERING — REMAIN SILENT TILL PERMISSION TO SPEAK IS GRANTED. But Simon Lent had not bothered to knock and he'd spoken as soon as he came into the room and strolled over to Macdougal's desk.

'You've often promised us that the punishment will be lighter if we own up to anything we do wrong, sir, and I want to own up to something now. I want to tell you so many things, Sergeant-Major, and I've got a lot of questions to ask you.' Simon Lent smiled and Macdougal suddenly felt cold because he seemed to see an old, bitter man watching him from behind the boy's blue eyes. 'May I start with the questions, sir?

'How would you react if you were suddenly thrown out of heaven and locked away in purgatory, Mr Macdougal? If you found your parents lying dead in a bath and a stranger claimed you? A stranger who forced you to remain in this hell-hole for brutes to torture while the teachers stood by and did nothing?

'Why did you stand by, Mr Macdougal?' He reached in his pocket and placed a small package on the desk. 'Did you resent me because I'm superior to you, perhaps?

'If that's true you are quite right, because I am superior, sir. I'm very intelligent indeed, and that's why Ray Denton died and Kathleen Clarke will never walk again. Why I may kill Sean Brady one day. Why you won't dare to stop me.' He pointed at the package and tittered. 'I've brought you a keepsake, Sergeant-Major. A gift that'll make you squirm for the rest of your life and remain as silent as Ray Denton's ashes.'

'I didn't say a word, Colonel Vayne.' Macdougal unlocked the deed-box. 'That boy's eyes hypnotized me and when I opened his damned parcel I saw that he was right. Simon Lent had me by the short hairs and I just sat there and listened while he giggled and cackled and told me how he'd doped the sweets and made sure Denton stole them. I kept my mouth shut, and I think you'd have done the same in my position. Simon Lent was a bit of a mechanical genius and he'd bugged my room with a microphone and an electrically operated camera.' Macdougal took a photograph from the box and held it out for Vayne's inspection. 'That's how my puir, bonnie Kate looked before the lorry crushed her. Do I need to tell you who the fella is, surr?'

'You do not, Donnie, and what a randy old goat you are! How exceedingly disgusting.' Vayne expressed disgust with a snort, but once again his emotion was tempered by envy and he rather wished that he'd entered the teaching profession. The girl in the snapshot was not merely bonnie, and she certainly hadn't been pure as Macdougal pronounced the word. She was strikingly beautiful and as naked as Eve before the fall, though she hadn't fallen on to the mat in front of the gas fire, Donald Macdougal's fire. Kathleen Clarke was stretched out alluringly, welcoming her elderly lover with zest: open arms, open mouth and legs; open everything.

'I congratulate you on your taste and your virility, R.S.M., but you don't deserve any compliments for morality, discretion or presence of mind.' Vayne snorted a second time. 'I presume Lent told you he had kept the negative of this and a copy of the tape recording. As you phrased it so aptly, Simon Lent had you by the short hairs and this piece of pornography could have sent you to prison if the police had got a squint at it.

'Yes, I appreciate the need for silence and I might have been equally docile in the same circumstances. But not for

long, Donnie Macdougal, and I've a few questions to ask.'
He scowled at the male figure displayed on the exhibit and
then threw the photograph on to its owner's desk. 'You're
a hard man, Donnie. You can discipline soldiers and teen-
age hooligans and you're a born killer without an ounce
of conscience or mercy. So why didn't you order those
louts to torture Lent till he handed over the evidence?'
Vayne nodded at the bonfire builders on the playground.
'They'd have enjoyed torturing your blackmailer, Donnie.
They'd probably have killed him if you offered 'em a
higher share of the profits.'

'A notion which I considered, surr, and rejected because
bairns tend to be talkative and a more practical solution
occurred to me.' Macdougal replaced the photograph in
his deed-box. 'There was an adult who couldn't talk because she had nearly as much to lose as meself, you see.
A young lady who was careless enough to allow Simon
Lent into a laboratory storeroom and steal the dope that
put paid to Kate and Ray Denton.

'The lady was also the only person Simon Lent didn't
actively dislike and I scared the living daylights out of her.'
He smiled at the recollection. 'I told Betty Smith that if
she couldn't put a stop to Simon's threats, I'd write a wee
note to her boss and the newspapers.

'A demand that was heeded, surr. Young Betty promised
to play ball, though her help wasn't necessary. The train
crashed, Simon Lent cleared off to sea, and I only keep that
picture as a reminder of the happy sessions I had with
Katie Clarke. I believed Lent was dead till you …

'What is it, Nolan?' He paused and raised his voice
because the boy accused of wasting solder had rapped on
the door and entered the room. 'I told you I had private
business to discuss with this gentleman, so what's amiss?
Trouble in the class – sinful idling?'

'Of course not, sir. We're all sticking to schedule, but

Mr Wolfe's secretary asked me to give you this.' The messenger held out an envelope. 'Came by special delivery ... could be urgent.'

'Thanks, son.' Macdougal glanced at the address and nodded. 'Go back to your work and I'll be along to check it when me business is completed.

'Now, who sent me this?' Macdougal's tone was unemotional as the boy walked away, closing the door behind him and his fingers were quite steady as they ripped the flap from the envelope. But after he had taken the letter out of the envelope, he changed. The whole of him changed. His body seemed to shrink and grow older. His eyes dilated, his face whitened, and his hands trembled. He leaned against the desk to support himself and for a moment Vayne imagined he was about to faint.

But only for a moment. The recovery was even more spectacular and sudden than the collapse and Sergeant-Major Macdougal laughed. A great, booming laugh that thundered around the room like a drum.

'Yer said that I was a born killer, Colonel, and you're right. I must have killed about a hundred men in my time, and I enjoy thinking about 'em.' He had finished reading the letter and marched back to the cupboard. 'And I was right in saying that we're two of a kind, surr. A pair of rotten apples who daren't split on each other because we're fighting a common foe. You've got your trains to protect and I have to preserve my good name and me liberty. You have to catch a saboteur and I want a roll of cassette tape and a film negative.

'Simon Lent was also right when he said I'd squirm, Colonel. I've squirmed for three years, but that's over now. Our wishes are going to be granted without any blabbing to the polis. I'm going to settle this matter nice and quiet and easy and I'll show you how.' He lifted a heavy metallic object from the drawer and crossed to the Bible. 'Oliver

Cromwell was equally right when he told his troops to put their trust in God and keep the powder dry. Cromwell was a soldier like us, surr, and old Donald Macdougal has a God he can trust.' He laid the letter beside the Bible and grinned. 'The Lord of Hosts has delivered the enemy into our hands.'

Eleven

'I have examined William Smith as thoroughly as time permitted, gentlemen, and he has received the Halsey-Borhein reactive tests and answered the emotive questionnaires compiled by my friend and colleague, Professor Emil Ranier of the Sorbonne.' Dr Margaret Puxton sat at the head of the table, as was fitting and proper in her view, and she considered the justice of Women's Lib while addressing her audience. Four boorish dullards lacking intelligence, respect and decent manners.

'I won't bother you with technical data which may confuse you, but each test and questionnaire has strengthened my earlier suspicions and here are the findings.' She paused impressively as though preparing to announce a cure for cancer or the source of perpetual motion, but the gesture failed.

Ted Morcom was calculating whether he could afford another addition to his doll collection, and Inspector Mason and Mr Emrys Evans had more serious problems on their minds. Should a description of Simon Lent's probable appearance be issued and a general call put out for him? Should the unions be told that there might be a train wrecker at work? Difficult decisions, but Archie Vayne had already planned his course of action and only two things worried him. Why hadn't Betty Smith contacted him to explain her behaviour in Kahn's office? When would Donald Macdougal ring?

'Aren't you interested in hearing my report on William Smith, Colonel?' Margaret Puxton winced because the chief offender had belched and a cloud of stale beer and cigar smoke was drifting around her. 'Do you find medical science boring or merely incomprehensible?'

'I am exceedingly interested and agog for enlightenment.' Vayne stifled a second belch. There was no point in offending the woman, but what a fool she is, he thought. Morcom had spoken to young Smith after his last session with Maggie Puxton and he and Evans and the policeman all knew what had taken place. Maggie Puxton had first thought that the boy was normal, but she had changed her tune, and hoped to prove he was as batty as herself. Maggie was a fanatical Freudian, but he had nothing to do till Macdougal telephoned him and he might as well listen to the rigmarole and have a few laughs at her expense afterwards. 'You have our full attention, Madam, so do proceed.'

'Thank you, Colonel Vayne.' She donned a pair of granny glasses and consulted her notes. 'I shall start by saying that you can forget about Simon Lent, gentlemen.' She was pleased to see Morcom nod approvingly, but her statement had not caused the gesture. Morcom had merely finished his mental arithmetic and decided that the doll could be purchased. 'Simon Lent may have been responsible for the original derailment three years ago. He may be dead, he may be in Australia, he may be anywhere in the world, but he was not on the Crematorium Bridge the other night. Lent is a product of the imagination. He exists in a sick man's mind.

'The distressed, guilt-ridden mind of William Smith, gentlemen, and I will try to explain briefly and simply how a guilt complex acts.' She did try, but the explanation was far from brief and guilt was not the only complex involved. According to Margaret Puxton, Billy Smith was a mass of neuroses, a swarming ant-heap of mental illness.

'*Fixation ... morbid identification ... self-hypnotization.*' The phrases poured glibly out and Vayne lit a cigar and glowered at her in fixed, morbid irritation. Whatever Maggie Puxton might say, Simon Lent was on the rampage and Billy Smith was not insane. Billy could have experienced some guilt when Simon ran off to sea. He might have suspected that Simon was responsible for crippling his father, and he'd admitted feeling nervous when they put him in charge of the evening Belle.

But Billy had seen Simon on the bridge. He must have seen him and the facts outweighed any psychiatric twaddle. The Colonel stood up and paced backwards and forwards across the room. Simon Lent was a monster who had stolen prohibited drugs to kill a boy and paralyse a girl for life. He had blackmailed a schoolmaster by bugging an office with a microphone and a camera. He had boasted of his achievements.

Past achievements, but more recent evidence was available. A heroin addict had died from an overdose and Simon Lent had written three letters. Two phoney suicide notes and one threatening demand which was quite genuine and must be paid in full, though not by the recipient, not by a debtor. The creditor would close his own account and that would be that. No more murders, no more missiles thrown from bridges, no more attacks on the 9.15.

Best of all, no more worries for Colonel Archibald Vayne and his footsteps quickened. 'I trust I'm not disturbing you by moving about, Dr Puxton, but a bit of exercise helps me to concentrate.' He knew that he was disturbing her and the knowledge pleased him. Very soon the phone would ring and he could prove that Maggie Puxton was a charlatan. It was a pity that he would never be able to reveal the source of his proof, but loyalty came before pride. A promise is a promise, an Englishman's word was his bond, a friend in need is a friend indeed. A friend who would settle the score and might be settling it now while Maggie Puxton droned on about compulsive guilts and emotional lesions. Regimental Sergeant-Major Donald Macdougal with a hundred corpses on the score-board. Please God Donnie increased his total soon.

'As a medico, I'm sure you'll agree that physical activity stimulates the old grey cells and *mens sana in corpore sano* is a sound tag, Doctor.' Vayne came to a crashing halt beside the window. 'Though your theory is a bit complicated for laymen to appreciate fully, I think we've got the general gist, eh, Ted?' He smiled and winked at Morcom. 'Dr Puxton believes that because Billy Smith and his sister feel responsible for former tragedies, they went gaga. Because Simon Lent was persecuted at school and old Smith was crippled in a railway crash the brain wheels started to creak and grow rusty, and other senses suffered accordingly. That Billy's eyes deceived him five nights ago and Betty's hearing was faulty. That the sins of the father were not only visited on his children, they possessed the children and Billy Smith became Dad. Old Peter Smith saw Lent on the bridge, gentlemen, and we're up against an unholy trinity.' He winked again and saw Mason and Evans smile back at him. 'An imaginary union of the beloved father and the prodigal son. The grieving mother and daughter; the problem nephew.

'If you can swallow that, my friends, you'll swallow anything.' Vayne emphasized his contempt by turning and staring coldly out of the window. The rush hour was over, the crowds in the station were thinning and fewer trains were leaving the platforms. Eight o'clock, and the clock above the booking office made him think of a quotation. 'And you shall hear the stroke of Eight, but not the stroke of Nine.'

That was Housman, but Kipling had outlined the situation more accurately: ' ... all unseen Romance

III

brought up the nine-fifteen.' Far more appropriate and how did the rest of the verse go?

> By dock and deep and mine and mill
> The Boy-god reckless laboured still!

Extremely appropriate, though the Boy-god wouldn't labour for long. The boy was a back number and today's 9.15 would glide safely down to Lythborne with two stolid, unromantic men at the controls. Archie Vayne's troubles should soon be over and Dr Sigmund-Maggie-Puxton-Freud had better have her own head examined.

'But if our medical adviser is right, we may have a lot on our consciences, gentlemen.' He turned and frowned at his male colleagues with mock disapproval. 'William Smith is obviously a dangerous character and I'm surprised that you haven't put him under lock and key already, Inspector Mason. Hell's bells, we've all seen him and read about him, and we know how his mind works.' Though Vayne was becoming worried that the phone might not ring, he chuckled because a really cutting insult had occurred to him.

'Yes, Dr Puxton, we've all seen *Psycho*.'

'Aye, they're here, lad. One thousand quid in used fivers, but I've got some questions to ask before I part with 'em.' Donald Macdougal spoke loudly into the telephone with a hand muffling his free ear. Though the study windows were closed, the school's annual Guy Fawkes party was in progress, and the sudden bangs and whooshes of fireworks made conversation difficult.

'Your letter stated that you'd ring me at eight sharp and it's almost a quarter to nine already.' He glanced at the note on his desk. 'Well, time may not matter, but good faith does so why should I trust you? I can't remember your handwriting and your voice sounds different. How do I know that you are Simon Lent and not some cheap confidence trickster impersonating him?'

'Of course my voice is different, sir, I haven't spoken to you for over three years and I'm ill, Sergeant-Major.' The earpiece rattled as the words were interrupted by a fit of coughing. 'I'm sick and desperate and you must trust me because you know that I've got enough evidence to jail you. I sent you a sample in the envelope.'

'That's true, but photographs and cassette tapes can be duplicated more than once.' Macdougal smiled at another alluring picture of himself and Kathleen Clarke displayed beside the letter. 'If you've taken copies, lad, what's to stop you squeezing me for ever?'

'I won't be here for ever, and I'm not a lad, sir. I'm a sick dying man and I couldn't call you before because I'm on the run, or soon will be. You won't have heard about Sean Brady, sir, but he's dead and I killed him like I killed the others.' Another sound rattled down the line, but Macdougal couldn't tell whether the speaker was laughing or sobbing. 'The police may not have connected me with Brady yet, but they will before long. They'll start looking for me, and that's why I must have money to get out of England. Money which you'll give me, Sergeant-Major, because if I'm arrested I'll see that you join me.

'Your trial should make interesting reading, sir. Kathleen Clarke was only fifteen when you first laid her, and I can imagine what the newspapers will say. "Schoolmaster perverted a child in his care." "Betrayal of Trust", "Criminal Enticement". Even murderers are disgusted by that sort of thing and I don't suppose you'll enjoy your spell in jail. You probably won't even come out alive.

'Sorry about that, sir.' He had coughed again and apologized. 'As I said before, I'm sick and dying, and you've got to believe me. All I want is to die free and there's no need for either of us to worry about the law. A thousand pounds isn't much to pay for liberty, and I swear that the only evidence against you is in my pocket now.' The caller was speaking from a public booth and a coin clanked through the slot as the time pips sounded. 'Evidence which can destroy you though, sir, and if you don't pay up, you'll be stuck up. Stuck in a dock, stuck in a prison with convicts beating you up while parsons preach sermons about you. As a Bible reader you should be able to think of a few appropriate texts. How would you fancy this one, Mr Sergeant-Major? "Better for him that a millstone be hanged around his neck"?'

'Very well, Simon. You've made your point and I'm prepared to do business and hand over the money.' Though Macdougal forced himself to sound defeated he was smiling at a wad of papers held together by a rubber band. Two genuine five-pound notes with trash sandwiched between them. Toy money which he had removed from the younger children's play shop. Worthless money but good enough for a blackmailing murderer, and if all went according to plan, the blackmailer wouldn't even touch it. 'There's no need to humiliate me, however, Simon, so please tell me when and where we shall meet and finish the transaction.'

'But I like humiliating you, sir. Your humiliations remind me of my own, you see. And talking of reminders and former times, I've got something to jog your memory.' The human voice stopped and Macdougal heard voices recorded by a machine. A girl's voice expressing false modesty, and then his own voice. 'Come on, Katie luv. Stop messing about and pretending you don't want me. Pull your drawers down and we'll get started.'

'Not very edifying, sir, but easily erased from the tape I'm going to give you.' The man's voice returned and Macdonald knew that it was the voice of Simon Lent: the same accent, the same hint of hatred, the same mixture of unhappiness and smug superiority. 'Easily wiped away and forgotten, Mr Macdougal, and if you have a pen ready I'll dictate my instructions.'

'I'm ready, Simon.' Macdougal lowered the hand from his ear and tried not to laugh while he noted the route and the meeting place. He couldn't have thought of a better place himself and everything was going his way. 'That is quite satisfactory and I'll see you in approximately twenty minutes and bring the money with me.

'Goodbye for the present.' He replaced the phone on its rest and then he did laugh. He laughed as loudly as he had done when he showed the heavy metal object to Archibald Vayne, and it was the same object that caused his laughter. Such a solid comforting thing. The very feel of the metal made him roar with mirth and when he stopped laughing he burst into song.

> 'Scots, wha hae wi' Wallace bled,
> Scots, wham Bruce has oftimes led … '

His favourite ballad and he bellowed the words while he struck a match and laid the photographs in an ashtray.

> 'Welcome to your gory bed
> Or to victory.'

'Or to victory.' He repeated the verse as the match caught and the prints curled, darkened and flared. There was going to be a victory and a gory bed, but no Scotsman would stain the bed sheets with blood.

Simon Lent would.

Twelve

A fair display and little hooliganism so far. Macdougal nodded approvingly as he left the building and crossed the playground. The school Guy Fawkes party was in full swing: Catherine wheels whirring, Roman candles showering sparks and crackers banging loudly. An impressive waste of gunpowder which evoked several attractive images in his mind.

The children capering around the fire made him think of imps tormenting lost souls in hell. The soaring rockets and ear-splitting thunder flashes reminded him of battlefields, and he'd done some memorable things during battles. How the Italian captain had screamed when the bayonet dug into his stomach, and the screams had been caused by surprise as well as pain. *Il Capitano* was hoping to surrender and his hands were above his head when Macdougal lunged at him.

The Korean gunners had been equally astonished when he came up behind them, but they hadn't intended to surrender. At least he didn't think so, and he didn't wait to find out. His grenades had killed half the bastards and he'd finished off the wounded with a machine pistol.

War was full of surprises, and so was peace. He had been surprised when that homo corporal, Turnbull, blew his brains out in Vayne's office and he was equally surprised now. How could any human being, even a maniac, be so foolish, so trusting, so bloody innocent?

But maybe it wasn't innocence or foolishness. Perhaps the powers of good had possessed the evil-doer. Macdougal thought of his grim Calvinist childhood in Scotland. A bare chapel with not even a crucifix on the altar, and a ferocious, bearded elder pronouncing the same text he had quoted to Archie Vayne. 'The Lord of Hosts has delivered the enemy into thy hands.'

Aye, God was at work as always: wrathful, merciless, but just. God had punished him for that unfortunate affair with Katie Clarke. He'd squirmed and worried for three years and the very thought of the tape and the photographs had made him toss and turn on his bed at times. But now God had forgiven him and his worries would soon be over. The Lord of Hosts was smoothing his path and walking beside him. God had chosen the one night of the year when explosions passed unnoticed and selected an ideal place for private conversation. God had lured a fox into the net by His age-old method. *'Quem deus vult perdere, prius dementat.'* God's hand was at the helm and his own hand would not let God down.

Neither his hand nor his handgun. Macdougal fingered the big Russian .44 revolver stuffed in his overcoat pocket. An undeclared souvenir from Korea which he had never fired in anger and never would. Though he had once hated the man he intended to kill he felt no hatred towards him now. Do gamekeepers hate vermin? Do executioners become personally involved with their victims? Of course not, but the job must be done. Foxes and stoats and birds of prey have to be exterminated. Murderers and blackmailers and saboteurs should be destroyed.

And one murderous, blackmailing saboteur was going to be destroyed in the very near future. The clock on the crematorium chapel started to strike while he crossed the bridge and he checked its accuracy with the treasured silver fob-watch presented to him by his last regiment. Nine p.m. on the dot, and soon he could telephone Archie Vayne a second time and report that the mission was completed.

117

Or maybe he wouldn't bother. He had told Colonel Archibald Hector Vayne that he was starting out by calling him at the station and repeating a verbal cypher before ringing off.

'I shall scale Mount Nitaka within the hour.' Words taken from the Japanese order to attack Pearl Harbour and the pretentious choice of a pretentious, boastful man who was too full of himself. Why should he bother to inform Vayne that the mountain had been scaled? If he'd sweated for three years, why shouldn't Archie Vayne sweat through the night? Sweating might do the fellow good, both physically and spiritually. Teach him to humble himself before the Lord, and earn grace. To accept that he was a mere chattel – a tool in the hands of God.

'But what in buggery is goin' on here?' Macdougal had crossed the bridge and entered the cemetery when a movement brought him to a halt. 'What mischief are the two of youse up to?' He produced a torch and repeated the question, though there was no need. It was quite clear what the boy and the girl emerging from behind a tombstone had been up to, and Macdougal's righteous indignation rose to a crescendo. 'You, Alec Catteric … You, Laura Trant! Two young souls fornicatin' in the presence of the dead. How shameful and disgustin' … How rash and dangerous! Don't yer realize what a terrible thing it is to rouse the wrath of Almighty God?

'Pull down yer skirt immediately, Laura.' The torch was shining on a pair of plump thighs, and another emotion joined pious rage, though not for long. The Lord demanded both morality and service and there was work to be done. 'And adjust yer trousers, Alec Catteric, and hie back to the party. That bonfire will be cold by morn', but think of the other fire which has bin burnin' since the world was created and will go on burning till Judgment Day.

'Canna ye comprehend the sufferings your foul lust has caused Lord Jesus, Alec? Dinna ye ken the horror of eternal damnation, Laura?

'Nay, I suppose not.' He shook his head sadly. 'Yer just puir beasts of the field; so awa' wi' yer but remember that hell lasts for ever and I'll be alive in the morn'.' A diesel locomotive was pounding up the railway incline and Macdougal shouted his assurances as the culprits scurried off. 'Alive and with a cane in me fist and I'll expect yer outside me office at nine-thirty sharp.'

A lucky intervention, Macdougal thought after he moved on. Alec and Laura might have decided to wander around the cemetery when their fun and games were completed. To roam through the gloamin' which was reserved for him and Simon Lent. Reserved for God too and commemorations of God's power and suffering were on view everywhere: urns and crosses and mourning angels.

God's angels – stone angels – the angels of death as rigid as the corpses below them. The cemetery contained hundreds of motionless figures, but one of them had no right to be there and Macdougal saw that he had reached his destination. An Angel was moving.

Not much of a movement; just a slight ripple of hair in the breeze, but enough to tell him that the face beneath the hair was not stone though it looked as white as marble under the moon. Enough to make him reach for the pistol in his pocket, though he didn't raise it at once. He was a professional soldier and a crafty Scotsman who could bide his while. He listened to the pounding locomotive. He watched a salvo of rockets hurtle through the sky, and he waited for them to explode before taking aim. He studied the face of the angel, and he smiled because another quotation had occurred to him.

'Ill met by moonlight,' he said, and squeezed the trigger.

'*Psycho* may be a work of fiction, gentlemen, but the plot is based on real-life data and I can cite a dozen instances of phrenetic self-identification.' Though fifteen minutes had passed since Vayne picked up the telephone and told the caller he had dialled the wrong number, Margaret Puxton still resented his sneer and she continued to press her point. 'Have you heard of Kevin Wright, Colonel Vayne?'

'I imagine that we all have, Doctor. The case was widely reported.' Vayne yawned ostentatiously but his thoughts were racing. Donnie Macdougal had started out and soon the telephone would ring again and report a *fait accompli*. 'Kevin Wright pretended that his mother was dead and murdered her to preserve the fantasy. He also posed as a schoolboy, though he was twenty-three years old, mourned a non-existent brother, and pestered the fire brigade with false alarms. Tried and sentenced at Chelmsford Assizes in March 1976. I think he got away with manslaughter on the grounds of diminished responsibility, but that is neither here nor there.

'We are not interested in Kevin Wright or a character from *Psycho*, Dr Puxton, and I know that Lent is the man you have to find, Inspector.' Vayne turned to Mason, speaking confidently but not over-confidently. His worries should shortly be over, and if there was any justice in the world he would be praised and promoted, and hailed as the bright lad who spotted the villain from the word go and made sure that the trains ran in safety. Pleasant prospects, but he mustn't be too assured, too knowledgeable. If he hinted that Simon Lent had died, Mason might check the source of his knowledge and suspect that he was an accessory to murder.

'Don't ask me why I'm so sure, Inspector, because I can't tell you. Perhaps I have a touch of the second sight. Both my parents came from the Hebrides and the gift is not uncommon there.' He closed his eyes for a moment as though peering into the future. 'Also, though I lack Dr Puxton's academic qualifications, a military training taught me how to distinguish truth from falsehood, and I can assure you on one score.' He opened his eyes and regarded Margaret Puxton with sadness and scorn. 'I have interviewed William Smith myself, Madam. I have also spoken to his parents and his sister and, though naturally distressed at the moment, I'm convinced they're as sane, reliable and honest as ... ' He tried to think of an example of level-headed, reliable honesty and settled for the N.U.R. representative. Trade unions can be stepping stones as well as stumbling blocks on the road to power, so why not step on one? 'As our friendly adviser, Mr Emrys Evans.

'Furthermore, I visited Glendale School today and talked to two of the teachers who actually knew Simon Lent. Men whose opinions I also respect and trust.' Vayne thought of the men in question while delivering the lies. The miserable Stanley Wolfe who was unworthy of respect, and Donnie Macdougal who could be trusted only as long as it suited his own ends. He respected Donnie as a fellow egotist, who'd slit his mother's throat if it was necessary. He trusted him as an expert. A professional killer who could be relied on to carry out a simple murder with no danger to himself. But Vayne also knew that if a danger did arise he'd share it. If Donnie Macdougal was arrested he'd sing like a lark and Archie Vayne would stand in the dock beside him.

But there was no risk, no danger and the signal had been given. 'I shall scale Mount Nitaka within the hour.' Those eight words told him that the letter-writer had contacted Donnie and arranged a place of meeting. Vayne had no idea where the meeting place was, but that needn't concern him. In a few minutes the phone would ring again and another agreed signal confirm that Donnie had completed his mission of mercy. After a longer span of time, an hour or a day or a week, Simon Lent's body would be found and the peals of approbation commence. 'Smart fellow Colonel Vayne. Knew who the blighter was from the very beginning and if I was the P.M., I'd put him up for a knighthood.'

'I have also established that while Sean Brady was employed at Glendale Road School, he gave Simon Lent little reason to love him.' The undubbed knight stubbed out his cigar butt and listened to a firework explode somewhere in the distance. 'On the contrary Simon Lent had an ample motive to murder Brady, and everything I have learned, all my intuition has told me, makes it clear that Lent did kill him.

'As our medical adviser has stated, we have a case of mania to worry about.' He bowed to Margaret Puxton, the sort of bow a traffic warden receives after writing out a parking ticket. 'A maniac named Simon Lent has murdered and mutilated a great many people in the past and there'll be more victims of his vendetta unless you stop that vendetta, Mr Mason. A bent crusade directed against the family who adopted him, the school where he was persecuted, the train his father boasted about; humanity in general, I shouldn't wonder.

'Of course I'm aware that Peter Smith was not Lent's actual father, Doctor, but this is no time to play upon words.' Vayne glowered at the interruption and appealed to Evans for support. 'Your union members and the passengers in their charge are in danger, sir, and the danger will remain until Simon Lent is dead or under arrest, and I'm certain you accept my thesis.

'A boy derailed the Channel Belle three years ago and he made himself scarce and posted a suicide note from Australia. But he never committed suicide and his hatred hasn't diminished. He's back in England, he's murdered Brady, and he's had another go at the 9.15. An attempt which would have succeeded if Billy Smith hadn't kept his wits about him and stopped the train.

'But the next attempt may succeed, unless we use our own wits, because the boy's a man now, and though he's a lunatic, he's not a fool.' Vayne was enjoying his rhetoric and the words boomed grandly around the room. 'It took intelligence and cunning to trace Brady and fill him full of morphine to provide a scapegoat. A lot of intelligence and cunning and that's why we should show some intelligence ourselves and forget Freudian jargon. Any big-game hunter knows that there are only two ways to get a man-eater. You set a bait or flush him into the open.

'I prefer the first method myself, but the choice is yours, Inspector.' Vayne thought of an earlier triumph while he spoke. The tiger had been old, far too old to catch animals, so it had turned on man and man had turned to him; the Indian villagers had appealed to the British Raj for help and the Raj did not fail them. The Raj's representative was safely stationed up a tree with rifle at the ready and he'd fired as soon as the senile beast lumbered into sight before the drums of the beaters. Who was to know that his first shot had gone wide and the Terror of the Jungle collapsed from exhaustion and heart failure? His other bullets hadn't missed, because he had jumped down from the roost and emptied his magazine into the carcass when the beaters arrived. Expert shooting ... lungs, brain and heart penetrated and foot planted firmly on the toothless head. *'Rung Ho, Sahib.* May God shower you with honour and many fine sons, Major Vayne.'

Generous expressions of gratitude, though he'd never wanted a son, and more honours were in store for him, provided Donald Macdougal did his stuff, and he didn't show his cards too openly. Knowledge and intuition must be implied, but no definite data revealed and he avoided Mason's next question.

'I can't tell you where Lent procured the heroin to kill Brady, but doubtless such trivialities will be cleared up after you've arrested him. An event which should come soon if you bait a trap or flush our tiger into the open.' He paused as a light flashed above the station roof and was followed by a deep rumbling bellow. Too deep for any firework. A freak thunderstorm was breaking and he hoped it wouldn't interfere with Macdougal's aim.

'In my opinion, publicity is needed and this is what I suggest. First thing in the morning we should hold a press conference and issue a challenge to our tiger – our crazed saboteur.' There was a second flash, a second bellow and the sound of rain pounding on glass. 'If Simon Lent hears that William Smith has been returned to duty after an unfortunate error of judgment and will be in charge of the 9.15 tomorrow, how will Lent react? I believe he'll make another attempt on the train and you'll have him, Inspector.

'A bit risky, but one must grasp this nettle, danger, and the risks will be negligible.' An understatement, Vayne thought, glancing at his watch. Almost half-past the hour and the saboteur was almost certainly dead. At any moment, the phone must ring and announce that Macdougal's labour was over. A man's voice asking for a Miss Amanda Kerr and then apologizing for dialling a wrong number. But, though his scheme might be unnecessary, it was both clever and cunning and he almost regretted Donnie's intervention.

'Simon Lent might be described as a puppet, my friends, and the strings controlling him are revenge and hatred. Hatred for a particular group of people and a particular train, and he will wait for that train at a particular point, the Crematorium Bridge. He will wait long enough for your chaps to grab him, Inspector, because the Channel Belle won't leave the terminus on time. She'll remain there till her crew are given the all clear.'

'Sorry, Colonel, but I don't believe that even a loonie would fall for that kind of dodge.' The policeman shook his head. 'And, though I'm beginning to share your view that Lent has returned to England, a press statement would cause serious unrest, and there's no need to alarm the public before we've examined the facts and decided on a proper course of action.'

'You are in charge of the investigation, Inspector, and it is not my job to give you orders, *unfortunately*.' Vayne stressed the adverb. He had suspected that Mason was slow on the uptake, but not that he was an utter imbecile. 'I can demand that my trains are adequately protected, however, and you'd better decide on a course of action damned quickly.

'Will you take it please, Ted?' His ill-temper vanished because the telephone was ringing; Donnie's signal of success was coming through and he watched Morcom pick up the receiver. He waited for Morcom to frown and deny all knowledge of a Miss Amanda Kerr. He waited for him to accept the caller's apology and ring off. He waited in anticipation, but his hopes were over-buoyant.

Morcom did frown, but it was not the kind of frown Vayne expected, and he didn't ring off. His grip on the instrument tightened, his face reddened and when he spoke his words were slurred and indistinct and repetitive. 'Yes ... yes ... I understand ... same time ... same train ... same location; the Crem bridge. Different crew; more serious results.

'We'll be over directly ... soon as possible ... see you then.' Morcom removed the phone from his ear and everyone in the room heard the faint wail of ambulance sirens. 'You were right I'm afraid, Colonel.' He jogged the rest button up and down and then asked the switchboard to connect him with the car pool. 'Right, but too late. Simon Lent was alive and this time ... ' He waited for the connection and used a phrase which was an almost exact reproduction of Vayne's words to Billy Smith a few days ago: 'This time he's really gone and done it.'

Thirteen

The thunder and lightning had stopped, but the rain fell in torrents. Solid jets of water that hammered the ground and reared up from the dry earth like rows of steel spikes. Rain that had already soaked Archibald Vayne to the skin and was turning the railway cutting into a miniature river. Rain that blurred the tail lights of the Channel Belle before it rounded the bend and slid off towards Lythborne with a replacement crew on the locomotive and 312 passengers behind them. Nervous passengers united by shock, pain and anger, and a single topic of conversation. What had caused that sudden, terrifying jolt that had brought the express to a halt; breaking glass and crockery, bruising bodies and fraying nerves? Indignant passengers who would demand a lot of answers in the near future. Who was responsible? Who had blundered a second time? Who was going to take the blame?

'I said that no one is blaming you, Gurney, but speak up for Christ's sake.' Vayne bellowed at the driver who was still half-stunned by his experience. 'Did it look like suicide or an accidental fall?'

'It happened too quickly for me to tell, sir.' The man forced himself to raise his voice and he looked at the steep, brick-lined embankment above them. 'The rain hadn't started then and we was doing well nigh eighty when I saw him.

'I say *him*, but I don't know whether it was a man or a woman or a child. I don't know whether he was running or jumping or falling and I can't even be sure whether I

127

saw his face or the back of his head. I just caught a glimpse of someone shooting down that slope and I jammed on the anchors and reversed the transmission. Not my fault that I couldn't pull up in time.'

'I've already said that no one is blaming you, Gurney, so stop worrying, and ask the police to drive you home. Then knock back a bottle of Scotch which I'm sure one of these newshounds will pay for.' He watched the man walk away and turned to a group of reporters. 'Two people are to blame, ladies and gentlemen, and one of them is the chap who's paid to keep that barrier in a secure state of repair.' He pointed at a gap in the fence topping the embankment. 'The timbers were obviously loose or rotten and the idler responsible for their condition will have to answer to me personally.

'The second culprit will probably be answering to God now, and humanity is well rid of him. We don't know whether his death was accidental or deliberate, but I do know that he was a criminal lunatic with a grudge against trains. However, this is neither the place nor the weather for an interview, and if you care to call at my office at eleven o'clock tomorrow morning, I should be able to give you the full story.' Vayne had been about to say more, but he had seen Mason scramble down the embankment and beckon to him. 'For the present, I'd advise you to follow Gurney's example. Go home, change into dry clothes and have a few large whiskies if you want to avoid a dose of flu. I shall be taking similar precautions very shortly.' He gave the journalists a hearty, man-to-man smile and moved across to the Inspector who had been joined by Margaret Puxton. 'Case closed, eh, Mr Mason? Lent's saved you the trouble of arresting him and he's also saved Her Majesty the expense of keeping him in prison for the rest of his worthless life.'

'I hope you're right, sir, but I don't think the case is

closed.' The policeman pulled out a handkerchief and dabbed the raindrops blanketing his eyes. 'I've been examining that fence and the wood wasn't loose or decayed, as we thought. The cross-pieces appear to have been weakened deliberately. By an axe or a hammer, or ... '

'Or by a boomerang hurled by an exceedingly powerful Australian aborigine.' Vayne guffawed, but his laugh was forced. If the police started to suspect that a third person might be involved, he and Macdougal would be in trouble and the possibility must be ridiculed immediately. 'You surely don't consider that the man was murdered, Inspector, when the facts are obvious, and we've already discussed Lent's character and know what his motivations were. A homicidal fixation directed against trains and the people on them. That's why I was certain it was Simon Lent who had fallen or thrown himself on to the line after Morcom repeated the phone message.

'Not that I deserve any credit, of course, and I apologize for my joke about the boomerang, Inspector. You may be right, just as Dr Puxton was right.' He bowed to both his colleagues and there was no mockery in the gesture this time. Goodwill was required to save him and Donnie Macdougal from a building which encyclopaedias described as 'lofty and imposing with vaulted ceilings and brilliantly coloured frescoes'. London E.C.4, the Central Criminal Court—the Old Bailey.

'My first belief was that Simon Lent had been watching the trains he hated when the fence collapsed under his weight, and he fell accidentally. My second notion was suicide and it's the only one that fits. As the doctor told us, Lent suffered from a guilt complex, so isn't it likely that his guilt became unbearable—rats gnawing at his soul as they gnawed the body of his last victim, Sean Brady?' Another lie because Dr Puxton had said nothing of the kind, but like many women she liked being proved right and nodded back at him.

'And if a guilt-ridden lunatic intended to kill himself, mightn't he have staged an accident to conceal suicide? Weakened the fence himself, thrown himself through the timbers, braced himself to take a header down on to the train?'

A header. Vayne savoured the phrase, though it usually appeared in soccer parlance or references to minor mishaps. 'The centre forward headed the ball in.' 'Old Jones slipped on a banana skin and took a header.' Not really applicable in this instance, because Simon Lent hadn't got a head. The locomotive's rail bar had severed his neck and its wheels had crushed his skull before the coaches rolled over him. No one would ever know how many other wheels and bars had mangled his limbs, his torso and obliterated features and fingerprints. No one could guess that Lent had been dead or dying before the train hit him. Who would look for a bullet wound in such a mass of offal?

But perhaps there hadn't been a bullet. Vayne's colleagues appeared satisfied with his explanation and he pictured the scene while the three of them walked towards the cars and ambulances parked on a stretch of empty ground beside the track. If Donnie Macdougal had known that the fence was rotten he wouldn't have used his gun. If he'd weakened the barrier himself, bargaining and blows would have sufficed.

'Aye, Ah've brought the sum yer demanded, lad, but Ah want ter check what Ah'm buyin' before partin' with it, Simon.' Vayne could hear the Scottish accents with the howl of a train like background music behind them. He could see Donnie reach for Lent's exhibits with one hand and hold out his wad of toy money in the other. He could see the sudden kick or rush that had sent Donnie's blackmailer reeling through the fence and down the embankment, down into the path of the 9.15. Simple Simon Lent; strong, crafty Donald Macdougal.

'Yes, I think suicide disguised as an accident explains everything, my friends, and we can sleep peacefully tonight. The saboteur is dead, the strife is o'er, the battle won.' Vayne grinned complacently because there was no cause for worry. The policeman and Maggie Puxton were satisfied; Donnie Macdougal had played his aces and Archie Vayne possessed a poker face and a gambler's intuition. He opened the door of his car, shook his dripping hat before climbing in and then scowled.

Ted Morcom was calling him. Ted had left one of the ambulances and was stumbling towards him through the rain. He had been told to try to identify Lent's body from a photograph, but Vayne knew it was a hopeless task. Who could identify scraps of rags and bones, mangled tissue washed clean of blood by water? No features, no fingerprints; nothing but cat's meat ... Flesh and offal.

'I think you'd better have a look at this, sir.' Morcom, a mannerless pup at the best of times, leaned into the car spattering him with moisture. 'Maybe unimportant, but they found this wedged between the ribs and I'm wondering how Lent came to have such a thing on him.' He held the exhibit under the car's courtesy light for Vayne's inspection. A metal disc with part of an inscription still visible on the buckled surface. 'Why should the officers, warrant officers, non-commissioned officers and men of the Durham Fusiliers have presented Simon Lent with a silver watch, Colonel Vayne?

'Who is R.S.M. Donald Macdougal?'

Fourteen

'There's no doubt that the body was Macdougal's. Apart from his watch and a signet ring, portions of clothing have been identified.' Vayne had assigned the press conference over to Ted Morcom and he sat facing Billy and Betty Smith in the senior staff canteen at A.C.I.D. A long L-shaped room, smelling of coffee and air freshener and the faint tang of chemicals which permeated the whole building. A discreet room at ten in the morning, which was why he had welcomed Betty's telephoned suggestion that they should meet there. Not a soul within earshot of their window table and subdued piped music to screen conversation. Almost as discreet as the cemetery from which a man had stumbled to his death.

'Nor is there the slightest doubt that Macdougal was killed by Simon Lent, and I'll explain what happened, because you won't split on me: not in a thousand years.'

The Colonel smiled grimly while he delivered his explanation and he stuck to the truth as far as he knew it. He told them about the blackmail letter and how Macdougal had prepared to deal with the blackmailer. He told them about Macdougal's signal stating that he was setting out to meet the blackmailer with a wad of toy notes and a .44 revolver in his pocket. A revolver which had vanished.

But Donnie Macdougal's scheme and his gun had misfired, because the blackmailer didn't want money. Revenge was Simon Lent's aim and he'd prepared the ground carefully. For once in a while, Inspector Thomas

Mason was right and forensic experts had already drawn up a probable sequence of events. The fence timbers had been weakened with a hammer or an axe and Donnie had been standing with his back towards them when someone or something forced him back; back and down. Back over the edge of the embankment. Down to the wheels of the 9.15.

'Your cousin has murdered at least two people during the last week, Smith, and Christ knows how many more would have died if you hadn't spotted him on the bridge the other night.' Vayne watched the young man jerk his head nervously, but the gesture had no emotional or mental significance. He might have been suffering from wax in the ear or an inflamed throat gland.

'But we do know that he'll kill again, if we don't nail him, and I've no doubt who his targets will be. You and your parents and your sister, lad, and that's why I've put my cards on the table and come here to help you.'

A slightly distorted truth. Vayne would be happy to help the Smiths, but he needed help himself and he somehow knew that they could help him. Betty Smith had saved him from the wrath of Solomon Kahn and an assault charge because there were several skeletons in her cupboard. Little Miss Betty didn't want to talk to Kahn or the police, but she might talk to a sympathetic friend who knew about at least one of those skeletons. To Colonel Archie Vayne, the soul of discretion, who wouldn't breathe a word to Solly Kahn or the authorities.

Not that Solly mattered. He was finished, or soon would be if the *Daily Globe*'s leader writer was any judge. Vayne glanced at a copy of the article spread open on the table. 'SIR SOLOMON KAHN SOWED THE WIND AND HE IS NOW REAPING THE WHIRLWIND. In the opinion of this newspaper, a hundred million dollars is a small recompense for the suffering caused by A.C.I.D.'s criminal folly.'

Fair comment in Vayne's view, and though the canteen was a pleasant room, the building contained other rooms which were far from pleasant, but just as quiet because their occupants couldn't utter a sound. A.C.I.D.'s dumb animals were literally dumb, and they were also deaf and blind. Kikey Kahn's cure for all mental evils had worked too well and he was paying for his money-grubbing rashness.

Mental evils, Vayne thought. Pandora's box opening to release mischief around the world, and it was his job to close another box and put a stop to more mischief. He had to slam the lid shut and he was becoming confident that he would do so before the day was out. That Simon Lent would be back in his box when the next evening the Channel Belle pulled away from Trafalgar Road Terminus for Lythborne.

'Yes, you're the targets, Billy and Betty,' he repeated. 'The whole Smith clan are on Simon's death list, and I doubt whether the police can stop him because he's got Macdougal's gun now.' Vayne nodded at two unobtrusive men drinking tea at the canteen counter. 'Your house is being watched, your parents will be followed if they go out to the shops or the pub or take a stroll in the park. The rozzers are doing their best to protect the four of you, but I wouldn't rely on them, Billy Boy.' He smiled maliciously as Smith's head jerked again. 'I wouldn't insure you for a brass farthing, unless you're prepared to defend yourselves.

'Simon Lent's got a hold on you, and I think you're covering up for him as you did in the past. You knew that he was blackmailing Macdougal, Billy, and you must have known that he'd stolen a quantity of Terapadorm S from this factory, Betty.' As Vayne watched the two young faces, he seemed to see the girl's features shrink and grow old, as they had done before. 'But there's more to it than that. I believe that you know where Lent may be hiding, but you're too frightened to reveal his hiding place. Scared stiff of what he might tell the police about you.

'Well, I'm not interested in what you did, Billy, and you can trust your Uncle Archie. The police won't listen to a homicidal maniac, and all you need worry about is homicide. Unless you help me, Simon Lent is going to kill you and there's nothing worse than death.'

'There are many worse things, Colonel; supernatural possession for example.' Though Billy Smith's tone was rational, his eyes were intense and Vayne knew he had won and the boy had reached breaking point. 'The police can't stop Simon, because he's not a human being and he's not in one place. Simon's here and there and everywhere, and he's probably listening to us now. I'll tell you about him, but I want a promise first. Will you swear by the spirit of your dead wife that you won't breathe a word of what I'm going to say to you?'

'No, I'll tell him, Billy.' Vayne had mortgaged Pam's soul without hesitation and the girl broke in, though she didn't look at her confessor. She stared into her empty coffee cup as an Indian fakir stares into an ink well to relive the past and read the future, and the past was returning. The coffee grains formed a face, the piped music changed to a human voice and the years slipped away. She was no longer in a factory canteen. She and Billy were standing in the front room of a terrace house near a railway line. She was watching the door of the room open. She was trying to draw back from the boy who came into the room with a school cap on his head and a satchel in his hand. She wanted to run away but her feet were nailed to the floor.

'I'm home, Betsy; home sweet home,' said Simon Lent and then he started laughing.

'Mr Macdougal is quite right, Billy. I am blackmailing him and I did kill Ray Denton, but it's not really my fault.' Simon Lent removed his cap and hung it up on a coat hook. 'You put temptation in my way, Betty, when you took me round the factory and showed me where the Terapadorm samples were stored. I couldn't resist pocketing a couple of them. I wanted to see how effective they were. That's why Ray died and why Kathleen Clarke is a paralysed imbecile. Curiosity and fun and a touch of malice to give the meal flavour.

'Past history though, and I don't need to ask what you're going to do about it. The answer is nothing, because Macdougal isn't the only person to be blackmailed.' He unbuckled his satchel and laughed again, the shrill, young voice twanging in their ears like the notes of a zither. 'I own you body, soul and mind. I can break up your happy home whenever I feel like it.'

The home had been happy, Betty thought while she blurted out the story to Vayne. Dad was a tyrant, the King of the Road, but you couldn't criticize him because engine driving was in his blood. Nor could you criticize Mum for her fits of migraine and depression; both her father and grandfather had suffered from them. Difficult parents, but she and Billy loved them. They all loved each other, and they'd been as close as any family could be till Simon Lent split them apart.

Simple Simon! She had tried to be fond of him in spite of his superior manners and his constant complaints and those long, hypnotic stares which seemed to penetrate her skull and probe among the brain cells as a dental instrument probes teeth for rot. They'd all tried to befriend Simon Lent, and they'd all failed, because he was incapable of love and friendship. An entirely self-centred individual who could give nothing.

But she hadn't believed he was an entirely evil individual

till he opened the satchel and produced his exhibits. A camera and a cassette; a photograph and a recording. That repulsive photograph of Billy and the girl. That repellent record of her own voice and the voice of her lover. Voices which Dad and Mum had heard when they came back from their evening walk earlier than usual.

Dad hadn't realized what the recording meant at first, but once he snatched up the picture he went wild. He had ripped off his belt and called her a foul-minded whore while he slashed at Billy. He'd told Simon that he'd murder him if he was still in the house when he returned from work. Dad delivered every insult and threat he could think of while Mum sat trembling on the sofa and sobbed, but the threats never materialized. When Dad came home it was to another house and the ambulance crew had to wheel him in. The shadow of a man with a scarred face and a broken body.

Simon Lent ran away. She thought he had died, but that was three years ago and she was wrong. Simon had also come back with his sneers and demands and his twisted mind. She and Billy had to kill him.

And they'd intended to. Betty's own mind didn't seem to be registering clearly, and though the distant past remained clear, the more recent events were hazy. Was it really Simon who had phoned again to arrange a meeting in the cemetery? Had he told her and Billy to splinter Ray Denton's gravestone as a sign of good faith?

'He didn't turn up, did he, Billy?' She looked at her brother for confirmation. 'We waited near the south end of the cemetery for over an hour, Colonel, but Simon never came. At least we didn't see him or hear him, though I seem to think he was there watching us.' Betty tried to relive that endless wait. The sound of the fireworks and the trains and the thunder. Lights flickering on the tombs, the end of the spanner protruding from Billy's jacket, and the brass studs of her handbag with the carving knife inside it. The constant feeling that they were not alone and Simon was very close to them. A dread which had increased after the rain started to fall and the lights diminished.

But would she and Bill have used their weapons if Simon Lent had appeared in the flesh, and would the weapons have proved effective? Only applewood stakes and silver bullets can harm a vampire. Could a knife or a spanner touch a werewolf—an evil spirit?

Unanswerable questions and she was talking to Billy and herself, because Vayne had lost interest. A waitress had crossed to their table and handed him a scrap of paper which was absorbing his full attention. A message which made him chuckle after he'd finished reading it and eased back his chair.

'I've no experience of vampires or werewolves or evil spirits, Betty,' he said, standing up and beaming happily. 'However, I told my assistant to telephone me here if he had anything definite to report, and it seems that he has. You and your brother may be disappointed that Lent failed to keep his appointment, but better late than never and we're going to visit him now.' He motioned them to follow him and walked towards the door.

'Simon Lent was hiding in the cemetery last night and he's still there. Like Sean Brady, they've just found him.'

Fifteen

The message was slightly inaccurate, because *they* hadn't found Simon Lent; Lucy Locket had. The previous night's deluge had obliterated any tell-tale footprints on the cemetery paths, and Inspector Thomas Mason and his men were about to give up the search when Lucy Locket, an Alsatian bitch with a keen nose, had suddenly whined and dragged her handler forward. Whines which had increased to frenzied barks after she reached a certain grave and sniffed at a speck of congealed blood beneath its carved inscription. Miss Locket earned a pat and an extra ration of horsemeat for her discovery. Tom Mason hoped to gain promotion and praise and he was holding an informal press conference of his own when Vayne and the Smiths arrived on the scene.

As it happened, Inspector Mason's hopes were unfulfilled, but they didn't matter, and Vayne hardly listened to him. The threats were over, the nightmare was past and the trains could run in safety

Simon Lent was dead. He had died shortly after Macdougal plunged down the embankment and he'd died with a dead man for company. He had crawled into a raised vault, 'Sacred to the Memory of Alderman Fetherstone Bussel – Philanthropist, Visionary, and Mayor of this Borough. Deeply lamented by family, friends, and fellow citizens. 1805–1905; a century in Christ's Service.'

'Yes, that's Simon all right.' A panel had been prised away from the tomb and Billy Smith peered at the thing lying beside the lamented alderman's coffin. 'He's put on fat, but his face hasn't altered, and we should have guessed that he might be here eh, Betty?' Billy drew back, but his sister didn't answer and he turned to Vayne. 'When we was kids, Simon discovered that the slab was loose and could be swivelled open and then closed from the inside. Fascinated by it, Simon was, Colonel, and he wanted to open the coffin too, but Betty and I stopped him. Said we'd screw him up with the corpse if he laid a finger on it. And maybe we should have done.' Smith spoke very slowly and his ashen features made Vayne think of a line from the Bible: ' ... a leper as white as snow.'

'What a lot of trouble that would have saved everyone, and ghouls and graves go together.'

'And you'd better pull yourself together, son.' Though Vayne snapped at the boy, his irritation was directed against himself and Mason because worry was returning and something was wrong. Several things were very wrong and he stepped forward as Mason gave an order and two ambulance men eased the body from its last hiding place. A stout, flabby body dressed in faded blue jeans. The body of a man who had died because there was a hole in his abdomen. A bullet had passed through the stomach wall, torn the intestines and he'd bled to death in the dark.

'If Lent had received medical aid in time, gentlemen, he might still be alive.' Mason resumed his lecture to the reporters. 'It would be interesting to hear the story from his own lips, but I can tell you roughly what occurred.' The Inspector was clearly enjoying himself and why not? The case had been solved; all was well with the world. 'According to the headmaster of Glendale Road School, Simon Lent was a sick individual riddled by hatred and Mr Macdougal was one of his chief aversions.

'For reasons which we'll probably never discover, Macdougal agreed to meet Lent near the embankment fence last night and, as I told Colonel Vayne, that fence had already been weakened. Simon Lent planned Mr Macdougal's murder carefully, and this weapon was found inside the tomb.

'Exhibit A, Constable Phillips.' Mason grinned triumphantly as the man held up a heavy, stub-nosed revolver, but Archie Vayne's irritation increased and he crossed to another constable who was listing the dead boy's effects. Everything was wrong because Simon Lent hadn't brought a weapon with him. The pistol was Donnie Macdougal's.

'However, Macdougal was a quick-witted ex-soldier.' The Inspector's smile grew wider as he watched the reporters taking notes. He'd be hailed as a quick-witted policeman in the evening editions, and it would be Superintendent Mason ere long. 'Before Macdougal reeled back through the railings, he managed to grab the gun and turn its muzzle against his attacker.'

'Following which Simon Lent also reeled back — back to his childhood hideyhole.' Vayne had finished reading the inventory and he sneered his objections. 'You're suggesting that Lent was a superman, Mr Mason? A superior being who walked more than three hundred yards with a .44 bullet in his belly? Who could pull aside a thick, marble panel and close it behind him? Who settled himself down to die like the proverbial wounded animal or a hero on a battlefield?'

The first example fitted Simon Lent, though a hero had died, and Archibald Vayne would always remember the hero with affection. Donnie Macdougal had won medals to prove his gallantry and he was cunning as well as heroic. Donnie hadn't twisted the revolver from his murderer's grasp. The revolver was his property and he'd shown it to a former commanding officer. He had also told his former officer that he intended to use the revolver after purchasing certain damaging items of information with dud money.

So why had Donnie been caught unawares and where were those items? Not on the embankment or the cutting or the cemetery, and not in the mausoleum of Alderman Bussel. Apart from the pistol and his clothing, Simon Lent had had few possessions. A bus ticket, a wrist watch and nine one-pound notes and fifteen pence in loose change. No photographic negatives or cassette cartridges to incriminate Macdougal. Nothing to embarrass Billy and Betty Smith and send them to another section of the graveyard and with other weapons. A knife in a handbag, a spanner in a pocket, murder in their hearts.

Vayne believed Betty's story, though he couldn't understand why a few dirty pictures should worry any sane person in this day and age. He couldn't understand why the girl had started to weep while the corpse was lifted on to an ambulance trolley. The body of a maniac who'd crippled her father, destroyed a train and caused her intense suffering.

But female emotions were as unpredictable as mania and the lack of evidence could be explained. Why should Simon Lent bother to bring the exhibits? He didn't want money, he wanted murder, and three victims were waiting for him. First Donnie Macdougal and then the Smiths, brother and sister. He must have known that Macdougal possessed a revolver and would have it on him. If Donnie hadn't fired at the same instant Lent released his own missile, a second appointment would have been kept and Donnie's weapon would have claimed further victims. Betty Smith would not be weeping and Billy wouldn't have stumbled off to retch behind a clump of yew trees.

Missile ... weapon ... the weapon of a boy. Though Mason was questioning him, Vayne was too excited to hear. Yes, that could be the thing that sent Donald

Macdougal reeling over the embankment. A simple weapon, a childish toy, but effective if the child had good eyesight and strong muscles: a catapult.

'I am asking whether you have a better explanation to offer, Colonel.' Mason had resented his sneers and he nodded at Margaret Puxton and a police surgeon. 'Though the time factors and cause of death cannot be definitely established without an autopsy, it seems obvious that Lent was killed by a bullet wound and that he died approximately one hour after Macdougal was struck by the train. So what are your objections?

'Mr Smith has told us that his cousin knew the grave could be opened and that it held a morbid fascination for him.' He watched Billy return from the trees with a handkerchief pressed against his mouth. 'If you doubt my theory, will you kindly let us know your own?'

'In a moment, Inspector, but allow me to ask you a question first.' Vayne hesitated because another piece of evidence had been revealed and his notion regarding the catapult was fading. He couldn't reveal that the revolver belonged to Macdougal. He couldn't repeat what Betty Smith had told him. He had to protect his own reputation as well as his trains and one of those trains had a departure time that tallied with a sum of money. Nine pounds and fifteen pence in a dead man's pocket. Twenty-one hundred hours and fifteen minutes; 9.15.

A coincidence, but there'd been such a lot of coincidences and a definite fact was staring him in the face as the trolley moved towards the ambulance. In the face, and from a face. From the peaceful, relaxed face of Simon Lent.

'Tell me, Mr Mason,' he said, knowing that all their joint theories were wrong and the truth was far more sinister. 'Have you ever seen a man smile while he was dying in agony?'

Sixteen

'I quite agree that a stomach wound is excruciatingly painful and the man must have been in agony before he died.' Though Vayne had questioned Tom Mason, Margaret Puxton answered him with her usual complacency. 'But after death the facial and bodily muscles would have relaxed and I would advise you to try to relax yourself, Colonel.

'Unless you have some private information which the police should hear about.' The last sentence had sounded like an accusation, but it had been followed by a handsome apology to William Smith. 'I am sorry that I had to subject you to those tests, Billy, and I'm delighted that my findings have been proved wrong. I imagined that you were suffering from over-imagination and guilt complexes, but your tension was perfectly natural under the circumstances.' Lent's body had been lifted into the ambulance and she smiled as the door was slammed behind it.

'However, all's well that ends well, and I am sure these good ladies and gentlemen won't bother you or your parents and will accept our official statement.' Billy and Betty and the journalists received the next smile; Vayne had received a frown. 'I presume that the statement will be issued very shortly, Colonel?'

Those words had been uttered seven hours ago and the statement had already been issued to the general satisfaction of almost everyone. Vayne and Morcom and a press officer had delivered their assurances and the clouds were lifted. It appeared that a man with an insane hatred against rail transport had been killed while murdering one of his former teachers. More information would be released after the autopsy and the magistrates' hearing, but there was no cause for alarm. The saboteur was dead ... the trains could run in safety.

Yes, almost everyone had been assured and satisfied, and the sole dissenter had confimed most of the assurances – Archie Vayne, who knew that they were a tissue of lies.

Simon Lent and Donald Macdougal were dead. That was a definite fact, and Maggie Puxton was probably correct in saying that Lent's smile was due to a natural relaxation of the facial muscles after death. But the manner of death was wrong and Vayne knew that as well as he knew his own name. As well as he'd known Donnie Macdougal, and he thought of Macdougal while he sat slumped in his office chair, yawning with tiredness because he hadn't slept for over forty-eight hours, and cursing his inability to tell the truth. The guilty secrets that tied his tongue and gagged a boy and a girl. He couldn't say that he'd known Macdougal's plans, nor could he reveal that Billy and Betty Smith had waited for Lent in another section of the graveyard. The confessions would make him an accessory to murder, and he wasn't going to stand in the dock for anyone; not even for a train, the Channel Belle that had crushed Donnie to pulp after he put a bullet through Lent's guts and reeled back down the embankment.

But why in the guts and why had Donnie reeled back? The man was an expert shot and he intended to kill his blackmailer quickly. Donnie Macdougal would never have allowed Lent to take him by surprise. If the boy had started to lunge at him, he would have blown his brains out and then collected the evidence and walked away. Safe as houses, free as air and not a visible stain on his tarnished character.

Donnie had been taken unawares, however, and he'd misfired because something had hit him at the same instant that he pressed the trigger. Something or someone, but not Simon Lent armed with a child's weapon as Vayne had once imagined. If Lent had had a catapult the police would have found it, though that meant nothing because they had found so little. No photographs or negatives, no cassette recordings, and no signs of a struggle against the fence.

No toy money either, and the Noes added up to a single Yes, which made Vayne forget self-preservation and reach for a telephone directory.

Simon Lent had had an accomplice.

'I fully appreciate your concern, sir, but I'm afraid that I am unable to help you.' The morgue attendant's name was Martin Sexton and it was entirely appropriate. His cheeks were shrunken, his body was lean and bent and his voice was mournful. He not only resembled his charges, he smelled like them, and Vayne tried to ignore the reek of formaldehyde and decayed gums. 'Don't think that I wish to obstruct you in the course of your duty, Colonel, but my own duties are equally heavy and these poor, dear people are in my care.' Mr Sexton was probably incapable of smiling but there was a touch of warmth in his tone as he looked at the metal doors lining the walls of the room. 'I regard myself as a sort of hotel-keeper, you see, and every man, woman and child within those cases is an honoured guest while they remain here.

'Guests to be treated with respect, sir, and it would be a breach of faith if I allowed you to disturb their slumbers.'

'Bloody hell, Mr Sexton. I only want to take a quick look at one corpse and I'm here in an official capacity.' Vayne reached for a cigar to stifle the objectionable odours and calm his temper. 'It is imperative that I examine Simon Lent and I've explained why.'

'Please moderate your language and remember where you are, Colonel.' Sexton pointed at a No Smoking sign with a claw-like finger. 'This is a sacred place and the dead are around us.' He watched Vane push the cigar back into his pocket and sighed. 'As I said, I would like to assist you, but I am not my own master. Before showing you Simon Lent's body, I would require permission from my immediate superiors, or Professor Alexander Chidle, the senior forensic officer for this area.'

'Then that solves our problem, Mr Sexton.' The Colonel laughed with false good humour. 'Alex Chidle happens to be one of my most intimate friends and if he was here he'd tell you to co-operate with me immediately.'

'But unfortunately he isn't here, Colonel. The professor is lecturing in Liverpool and he won't be back till to-morrow.' Though Sexton still hesitated, Vayne's claim to friendship with a man he had never met had impressed him and his tone became less formal. 'That's why the autopsy on Lent has been postponed, sir, and most unwisely in my opinion. Because the cause of death appeared obvious, the police surgeon hardly bothered to examine the cadaver, and I'll tell you this.' He leaned forward and Vayne forced himself to withstand the blast of polluted breath. 'Though I'm no doctor, I've handled a lot of corpses in my time, and there's something very odd about our recent arrival, Simon Lent.'

'I'm sure that you know far more about corpses than most doctors, Mr Sexton.' He had paused and Vayne prompted him with flattery. 'Where death is concerned you are the specialist. An expert, who is completely dedicated and devoted to his work, and it's your opinion that counts.'

'Correct, sir. I do understand the dead, and I can even

talk to them and listen to them sometimes. But it's not my place to criticize the medical pundits, and we'll have to wait for the professor's return.

'All the same ... ' He paused a second time and raised his eyebrows. 'We've met before, haven't we, sir, and your business was personal. Vayne ... Vayne ... Vayne?' He concentrated while repeating the name and the Colonel could almost hear his nerve fibres creaking. 'Yes, of course, you're the husband of poor Mrs Pamela Vayne. One of the first guests to be brought here after that dreadful derailment on the Lythborne line. Such a sweet and gentle lady; so very lovely.

'I was referring to the deceased's personality, sir.' He had seen Vayne wince and patted him on the shoulder. 'Though your dear wife was hideously mutilated, her aura remained; as fresh as a May morning, as fair as the Rose of Sharon. All spirits live on till their bodies are committed to earth or fire. The souls that do not die but wend their ways to heaven, hell or purgatory, and I can recognize them for what they were and will be until Judgment Day. The good and the bad – the blessed and the damned. I can scent them as a gardener breathes the fragrance of a flower. I can sniff them as a terrier noses out a rat.

'But have no fear, Colonel. Your wife is a good woman and, though you suffered a tragic loss, she's waiting to welcome you in paradise.' Mr Sexton was so carried away that he failed to notice Vayne shudder at the prospect, and then his sanctimonious manner altered and he grimaced at one of the doors. 'There'll be no paradise for that stiff, however. Simon Lent is a bad egg and he'll start to fry as soon as Professor Chidle has finished with his carcass.'

'Which is why I want to look at him, Mr Sexton.' Vayne's manner also changed and he tried to speak like a bereaved husband. 'My wife did die tragically and I believe that that man may have killed her. But though my personal grief is unimportant, there's a job to be done, and we can't wait for the autopsy. Unless you open that box for me, there may be more tragedies and I've explained what I want to know.'

A true statement, stretching the truth here and there, concealing the facts now and then, saving his own skin. But getting to the truth before Professor Chidle confirmed his suspicions and took the credit.

Simon Lent had not been alone when he met Donnie Macdougal by the embankment. A companion was stationed behind the fence, but he'd acted too slowly. Donnie had fired before Lent's friend stunned or killed him, pocketed his pistol and his toy money and rolled his body down on to the rails. Lent was dying when the confederate took him to his hiding place. Three hundred yards through the graves and along the gravel paths and across a square of ornamental spikes surrounding the tomb of a Victorian alderman. Rain falling in torrents and lightning flashing in the sky. Unless the third man was a fool and a giant he wouldn't have carried Simon Lent to the hideyhole. He'd have dragged him there and the proof must be apparent.

'You expect to see bruises and cuts and abrasions, Colonel, but I'm afraid you'll be disappointed.' Vayne's kinship with Pamela had won Sexton over and he unlocked the door. 'You can have a look at him, though your eyes won't help you. Apart from the bullet wound, there are no disfigurements to speak of.' The door was open and he slid out a tray covered by plastic sheeting. 'There is something very odd about this chap, however, and I'm surprised that the ambulance crew didn't notice it. Maybe they aren't used to handling dead weights like me, or perhaps they were just plain thoughtless.

'But you've been doing a lot of thinking, sir, and I imagine you're a strongish man.' He pulled back the sheet to reveal the stout, pallid body. 'That's Simon Lent, Colonel Vayne. I've broken my official regulations and my code of honour by showing him to you, and you can return the favour by showing me something in return.

'Show me just how strong you are, sir.' He stood aside and motioned Vayne forward. 'Show me how easily you can lift him.'

Seventeen

'He's dead, Dorothy, so aren't yer going to celebrate with me and have a drink?' Peter Smith hobbled to the sideboard, but his wife didn't look at him or speak to him. She was sitting on the sofa with her grey head bent over the gas fire and her eyes were glued to the five faces reflected above its jets. One face was her own and it was melting.

'Stop being a misery, lass, and let's see you smile. Simon's finished with and he'll not trouble us no more. Our Betty can sleep sound at nights and Billy should be back on the job tomorrow.' Smith unstoppered a beer flagon with his crippled hand, which felt much stronger than usual. His whole body seemed to be growing stronger. Even his legs had ceased to hurt him and he'd walked back from the pub without difficulty. The ghost was laid, the terror had ended, and the years were slipping away. Fear, as well as physical injuries, had caused his paralysis and soon he might be himself again. Strong, virile and confident; the King of the Road.

'Come on and get this inside yer, Dot.' He filled two glasses and carried them over to the couch. 'The least we can do is to toast our benefactor and here's to him.' He handed her one glass and raised the other. 'To Regimental Sergeant-Major Donald Macdougal.'

'To the man who was murdered, darling.' Dorothy Smith sipped at the beer, but she continued to stare at the fire. Another face was visible in the reflector now and its expression kept changing, though she couldn't imagine how or why or in what order. Had Macdougal been smiling or frowning when he reached the embankment fence and saw that Simon had kept his appointment? Had he laughed or gasped as he held out the money and fired his revolver? Had he screamed or shouted while he reeled down the embankment? Was he conscious as he lay on the rails, and heard the approach of the 9.15?

Unsolvable technicalities, but there were more important questions that had to be answered, and at long last Dorothy Smith forced herself to ignore the faces in the fire and look at her husband. 'Yes, Donald Macdougal killed Simon, Peter, but who killed Macdougal and who'll pay for his murder?

'Not you and I, my darling, though we're to blame.' She pointed at the painting on the wall. A family holidaying on a beach; the sea and the sand and the sun, the hills and the trees and the little white houses. 'Our children will settle the debt as they've always done, Pete. They'll suffer from your pride and my weakness, love. Betty living a lie that she was a hand in a factory. Poor frightened Bill, who dreaded driving trains.

'Do you remember what you said to Billy, when he was young, Pete? All that talk about speed records ... all those boasts and sneers that shamed him. All those filthy insults you shouted at him and Betty on the day of your accident while I just sat and sobbed and did nothing.' The woman stood up and kissed the man's scarred face. 'Yes, I'm as much to blame as you are, Peter. I insisted that we gave Simon Lent a home. I didn't suspect that a boy could be a monster; an evil spirit who wouldn't die.'

'But he is dead, lass, so stop your whining and forget about the bastard.' Smith took another gulp of beer. 'Lent's as dead as Macdougal and no one's going to suffer, because corpses can't talk.'

'The body is dead, Peter. It's lying in a mortuary, but

what about the others? Can't you understand that Simon
Lent was not alone; not a single unit, but part of an army?'
She paused and quoted with complete conviction. ' "My
name is Legion for we are many."

'That legion is still on the march, darling, and Betty
will never sleep in peace and Bill must never step on to
another locomotive. If he does there'll be a second crash,
because Bill won't see a boy on the bridge next time, and
he won't slow down for the Crem Bend. The demons will
possess his brain and he'll go roaring on to die.'

'Possession!' Smith flushed with anger. 'You're talking
rubbish, lass. There's no such thing as possession and the
only demon is locked up inside a morgue freezer. Of
course Billy is going to drive again because it's in his
blood. Our family have been main-line drivers for four
generations and you can't break a tradition like that.

'But what's the matter, Dot?' His anger changed to
concern because she had staggered away from him and
was clutching the mantelpiece to support herself. 'Are you
ill, darling?'

'You know that I'm ill, Peter. I've been ill for a long
time, but that's not important. I'm frightened, darling.
I'm scared out of my wits because we're not alone.' She
stared at the ceiling and shuddered. 'Somebody is moving
about up there.'

'There's nowt but the two of us in the house, lass, and
you've always suffered from imagination.' Smith had
listened for a moment, but all he heard was the tick of a
clock and the woman's breathing. 'You've always imagined things, Dorothy, and I'll have to put your mind at
rest as usual, so sit down, finish yer drink and wait for me.'
He walked to the door, trying not to drag his feet on the
carpet. Trying to pretend that his legs were not bothering
him, though pain had returned and elation vanished.
Trying to ignore his wife's fears and reassure himself.

There was no one moving about upstairs, because a corpse could not rise from the grave and the sleeping dead would never awaken. Simon Lent had had no confederates and he was done for. Soon Billy and Betty would return, but for the moment he and Dot were alone. Safe and secure and comfortable; snug as bugs in a rug; a loving couple.

'Aye, you're a strange girl,' he said, pausing in the doorway and creasing his lips into a smile. 'Wanton and fey and superstitious, and I was a fool to court yer, though I don't regret it, lass. Christ, how I love yer.'

'And I you, my darling.' The woman watched him shuffle across the hall and pity brought tears to her eyes because she knew that his confidence was forced and he was as frightened as she was. He'd been frightened since the ambulance brought him back from the hospital and he saw the big, modern house, and the new furnishings and the packing cases. The king was dead, but there was a prince who could not die. Who would haunt them for ever, unless ...

For ever ... unless. She finished her drink, but she didn't sit down. She listened to the weary footsteps climbing the stairs, she heard a bedroom door open and shut; she heard voices. Faint voices, but far more distinct than the telephone bell and they made her hurry to a desk and take something from a drawer. A thing which spoke to her while the telephone continued to ring and her eyes sparkled with joy as well as tears. Though men and women were defenceless against evil, angels could harrow hell and she knew an angel.

An angel with the power to wipe out fear and suffering and that angel was very close to her. The voices had ceased, the phone had stopped ringing, and Dorothy Smith hummed the nursery rhyme and listened to the footsteps returning down the stairs.

' "Once a lady loved a swine ... ",' she crooned and then she didn't say anything for several minutes. She stared at a man's face, and she opened her mouth and screamed.

Eighteen

'No more questions, Ted. Just do what you're told and see that those chaps keep their eyes skinned.' Vayne slammed down Mr Sexton's telephone, and then picked it up again, but hesitated before dialling another number. He had protected a train and the 9.15 was in no danger, provided Ted Morcom obeyed his orders. The Channel Belle could travel to Lythborne in safety because men would be stationed on the Crem Bridge and the embankments. Men waiting to catch a saboteur whose name was not Simon Lent.

Not if Sexton's suspicions were correct, that was. Not if his own brains and muscles and intuition hadn't deceived him, as might be the case. It was a long time since he had lifted a dead body, and he and Mr Sexton could be wrong. If they were wrong, Morcom and Inspector Mason would make him a laughing stock. That was why he had cut short Morcom's questions and said that the railway line should be guarded as a routine precaution. Simon Lent's death had aroused public interest and some child or vandal might be tempted to follow his example.

A reasonable explanation, and he'd done the job he was paid to do. The train was safe, and there was no reason why his conscience should trouble him. If Lent had had a crazy confederate who shared his hatred of the Smith family that was their bad luck, and he'd tried to warn them. He had phoned the house twice already and got no reply. He couldn't tell Mason that they might be in danger, or dead already. He had to play possum and protect himself and his reputation.

But there was no harm in trying to warn them a third time. Vayne twirled the dial, listened to the ringing tone for a full half-minute and then shrugged. There was nobody in the house; nobody alive to answer the phone, nobody to talk to. He was about to replace the receiver when he heard a click and a familiar voice. The voice of Betty Smith who laughed at his anxieties.

'We're perfectly all right, Colonel, and I can't imagine what's worrying you. Simon is dead and our worries are over.

'But I've only just got home, so will you hold on for a moment?' There was a longish pause and when the girl spoke again she didn't laugh, she stammered, 'Colonel ... Colonel Vayne. Can you come over here? Come now — come quickly. Simon wasn't alone when he killed Mr Macdougal.' Her voice rose and fell like gusts of wind. 'He had a partner and he's sent us another letter.'

The man who had killed Donald Macdougal walked slowly through the evening streets because he was tired and there was no need to hurry. He had caught a bus almost immediately and left it before reaching his destination. He had plenty of time. All the time in the world to think things out and plan carefully.

All the time in the world; all the time in heaven, hell or the void. He hoped it would be the void, because there was no place for him in heaven and he feared hell; or rather the people he'd find there. Simon Lent was in hell and so was Brady. Weak, stupid Sean Brady who had been too fuddled with meths to recognize him when he'd traced him to his drop-out pad. Big, brutal Brady who had shrunk in body and mind since their last meeting. A semi-corpse who had grovelled at his feet when he offered him a shot of heroin. A sub-human shambling away with his fix and his envelope and his load of stones to die amongst the rats.

Brady was no loss to anyone, least of all to himself, and giving him an overdose was a kindness. He had put Sean Brady out of his misery, but what about the others? The crippled and the dead, and those who were about to die. The boy and the girl on a motorcycle. Simon Lent had destroyed them, but there was a second girl; his girl – the girl on the bed.

A girl with a body rather like that. The man was in Soho and he halted and looked at an advertisement outside a strip club. Yes, very much like that, though the face was different and he couldn't remember her name: Betty or Bella or Belle. The name started with a 'B', but he wasn't sure how it ended and he turned away from the picture which was blurring before his eyes. So many things became hazy and blurred these days. At times his memory failed completely and he hardly remembered his own name or who he was.

But he knew what he had to do all right, and the knowledge had come to him like a vision, though there was no knowing whether the orders originated from God or the devil. The source was unimportant, however. Only the instructions mattered, and they'd been delivered so clearly and firmly. He had heard the voice as distinctly as he could hear the drone of traffic and the strains of a guitar twanging on the next corner. He had felt the fingers grip his arm as tightly as his own fingers were gripping the briefcase in his left hand. Clear, definite, logical instructions; signposts to lead him away from hell. His life had been a sort of hell, but soon he'd be free of it and he could afford to be generous.

The man withdrew his wallet and tossed a crumpled note in the guitar player's cap, and smiled as he walked on. The musician would regret the gift when he examined it, because it had come from Macdougal's wad of toy money, but he had no regrets and his earlier fears of damnation vanished. He was sauntering down the bright London street towards freedom; Wardour Street and Frith Street and the Charing Cross Road. Strolling along to the end of one journey and the start of another. His name and identity were unimportant. He'd be told who he was when the time was ripe and all he had to do was obey orders, as he'd done in the past. Brady was dead, Simon Lent was dead, and the Smith family were as good as dead.

He might be dead himself within an hour, but there was no defence against fate and what was written was written. Saint Paul had realized that on the way to Damascus, and so had Nelson while the *Victory* carried him to death and glory. The man had reached Trafalgar Square and he looked up and spoke aloud to the lonely stone figure on the column.

'Kismet, Hardy.'

Nineteen

'Come over quickly,' Betty Smith had pleaded and he was doing so. Archie Vayne had rarely driven faster because the girl had reason to be frightened and the knight errant was rushing to rescue a damsel in distress. Three clichés scribbled on a sheet of paper and pushed through a door flap had confirmed his theory. 'Birds of a feather flock together.' 'The gang's all here.' 'I'm dead, but I won't lie down.' Simon Lent had not acted alone.

Birds do flock together, and so do maniacs, Vayne thought while he hurried his Invicta through the thinning evening traffic. Betty seemed certain that the note was in Simon Lent's handwriting, but Lent couldn't have delivered it because he was dead, and his corpse was lying down in Mr Sexton's morgue. But though Lent's body had been weak and flabby he possessed a hypnotic personality, and before Macdougal killed him he'd made a convert to his cause. A religion of hatred which still flourished because the disciple was carrying on the crusade. Carrying it on, as he'd carried his master across the grave-yard. Sexton was sure that Lent couldn't have made the journey alone. He was equally sure that Lent couldn't have opened the tomb alone. He was almost sure that Lent could not have killed Macdougal. The disciple had done the master's bidding and he'd continue to serve the master till a knight errant put paid to him.

Birds of a feather flock together! How many birds were there? Though Archie Vayne prided himself on courage, he slowed the car slightly before turning into the long, suburban road leading to Peter Smith's house. Was there more than one disciple, perhaps? Charles Manson had recruited a regiment of murderous zombies, and Simon Lent could have done the same. Ted Morcom might find several fanatics stationed on the railway bridge. Other murderers might be waiting for him at the end of the road. Should he stop at a telephone booth and call the police?

No, there was no time to summon help. Betty and her family were in danger, and knights errant were immune to fear. Though Sergeant-Major Donald Macdougal had been taken by surprise, Colonel Vayne was prepared for action and Donnie wasn't the only person to own a gun. There was a target pistol in the car's glove compartment, and, unlike Donnie, he had a permit to carry it. He also knew how to use it and the bird or birds wouldn't fly at him. He'd let fly at them first and he'd shoot to kill.

A good soldier should show caution as well as courage, however, and reconnoitre the terrain before advancing. Vayne switched off his lights and ignition, put the gear lever into neutral and freewheeled silently past the big house which looked peaceful enough. A carriage lamp shone in the porch to welcome him and other lights were visible behind the curtained windows. All quiet on the Western Front, but the enemy might be waiting for battle, and Vayne checked that his pistol was loaded after he stopped the car and climbed out.

All quiet; too quiet; as quiet as a grave had been before Simon Lent was dragged into it, and Vayne's caution increased while he walked towards the desirable residence which Peter Smith's wife had purchased. Only a quarter to nine, but the entire area appeared dead and deserted. Even the stealthy tread of his footsteps seemed to disturb the peace, and he avoided the gravel drive and didn't go straight to the porch. An automatic warning device in his brain told him that danger lay ahead, and he tiptoed across the lawn and peered through a chink in the sitting-room curtains. As far as he could see there was nothing amiss, but what he heard confirmed his fears and he swung round and ran for the door.

A girl was whimpering, a man was chuckling and the knight errant had to rush to the rescue. He didn't notice a rose bush rip his trousers before he reached the porch. He felt no pain when he flung his shoulder against the door and its solid frame resisted his effort and he toppled back down the steps.

Brute strength was useless, but the damsel was still whimpering and her knight was amply armed. He pulled himself to his feet, released the safety catch of his pistol and pointed its muzzle at the door lock. He was about to fire and shatter the lock when the door opened and a puzzled face stared at him.

'What on earth are you up to, Colonel Vayne?' said Mrs Dorothy Smith.

'You believe that my daughter answered your telephone call and told you that she had received another threatening note from Simon Lent.' Vayne had explained his anxieties but Dorothy Smith was still bewildered and she nodded towards a tape recorder on the sitting-room desk. 'I'm afraid you are mistaken, Colonel, and all you heard through the window was the recording of a radio play. I've seen no letter and Betty isn't here. Neither of our children are here and apart from my husband, who is resting upstairs, you and I are alone in this house. Quite alone and Simon can't harm us any more. Simon Lent is dead, so do please put that thing away and sit down.'

'As you wish, Madam.' Vayne lowered his pistol, but he kept hold of the butt and he ignored her offer of a seat. Dorothy Smith was lying to him, and she was also terrified, though not of him or his gun or his attempt to force the door. That door had been opened and closed shortly before he arrived and she had had visitors. Though the recorder might have been playing, the tape was not a radio play. Though the house was warm, she was shivering and he could see beads of sweat beneath her drab grey hair. Though her glasses were almost as dark as her husband's, he knew that the eyes behind them were furtive.

'Then where are your children, Mrs Smith?' Vayne tried to speak normally but he shared her fears. Were the curtains moving because the window was partly open, or was someone stationed behind them? Had a floorboard creaked in the adjoining dining-room? 'I did speak to Betty less than half-an-hour ago and she asked me to come here.'

'How do I know where Betty is, Colonel? Probably with a man or a boy, I shouldn't wonder. A great one for the lads is our Betsy, though she keeps quiet about 'em. Dad and I never suspected a thing till Simon Lent came back from school with his horrible tapes and his foul snapshots. God, how angry Dad was and how God made him pay for his anger.' Her face was damp with tears as well as sweat now and they trickled down her cheeks like rain on glass. 'No, I don't know where Betty or Billy are. I'm not even sure where Simon is, though they told me he was dead.' She opened her lips and Vayne heard a sound which might have been a sob or a gurgle of laughter. 'I know so little, you see. For three years I've been playing a sort of game and living in a make-believe world. But it's got to stop now and that's why I asked you to come and help me. Why I said that Simon had sent another letter.'

'It was you I spoke to on the phone, Mrs Smith?' The jigsaw puzzle was fitting together, but Vayne had no idea what the final picture would reveal. 'You impersonated your daughter?'

'Of course I did, though maybe I was wrong. Dad told me not to talk to you for Billy's sake. He thought that you'd stop Bill driving and break the tradition.

'But I've gotter talk to someone who'll understand, and I think ye're a sympathetic chap, Colonel.' As had happened before her speech kept varying from the accents of Mayfair to cockney. 'Yes, I think you're a kind man at heart and Dad said that you've got your wits about you.

'Poor old Dad sleepin' away up there.' She clutched Vayne's arm and glanced at the ceiing. 'Or maybe he isn't asleep ... perhaps that demon's come home to wake him.

'No, that's foolishness and there's nothing to be frightened of. Billy and Betty are out, Simon's dead, and we're alone, Colonel. You and I and Peter Smith, the crippled king who can't hurt no one no more. A king and a fool, sir, and I've heard that the Russians say that there are two sorts of fools: the Summer Fool and the Winter Fool.' Her grip on Vayne's arm tightened and there was a trace of a smile on her tear-stained face. 'You can recognize the Summer Fool as soon as you clap eyes on him, because he's a boorish peasant dressed in rags and he runs about boasting with a straw sticking out of his mouth.

'But the Winter Fool's more difficult to spot. A big, self-important man, who comes to your door with snow on his fur cap and his frock coat and his leather boots. It's only after he's taken off the cap and the coat and kicked the snow from his boots that you realize he's a fool.

My husband is a Summer Fool, Colonel Vayne, and that's why he got bust with rock three years ago. That's why he's sitting in his chair now, and why I want to talk to you .' She released Vayne's wrist and moved to a desk. 'I told you the story of the lady who loved a swine, and I wonder if you'd be interested to hear another fairy tale and look at another photograph album. I've not finished the end of the story, but it starts in the usual way and there's a sound track as well as illustrations. Once upon a time there was a royal family. A king and a queen, a prince and a princess who did a very stupid thing.' She laid a book on the table, switched on the recorder and walked back to the desk. 'They took a court jester into their palace.'

Vayne wasn't sure whether the woman laughed or sighed as she moved away, though he hardly heard her. The first three pages of the book were innocent enough: wedding groups, christening groups and family groups, photographs of children and relatives and friends. But the fourth page was far from innocent and it sent the blood rushing to his head and all he could hear was the sound of the tape. The recording must have been made at the same time as the picture was taken and they both proved him wrong. The girl was not whimpering in fear of an attacker. She was giggling on a bed with her lover astride her body and her face contorted by lust.

An interesting spectacle which made nonsense of his theories, though the danger remained. Simon Lent had had no accomplice or disciple; Archibald Vayne no longer had a gun. The pistol had been snatched from his fingers and its muzzle was pressing against his spine.

'You're the Winter Fool, Colonel.' The tape had ended and a voice whispered in his ear. A strange voice which he didn't recognize. 'You're nearly as foolish as silly Dotty Smith who hoped to confide in you. Too foolish to realize that Simon Lent never asked Brady to deliver a letter.' A sheet of paper dropped on to the table and Vayne saw the same writing that had covered a note in a dead man's pocket. 'You're also a presumptuous fool, Archie Vayne, and you imagine you know what happened to the royal family: the king and the queen, the children and their jester.

'Wrong as usual, Winter Fool, but the family are waiting upstairs to tell their own story and we must go and meet them.' The pistol drew back and then jerked him forward. 'I hope you'll enjoy the meeting, Archie Vayne; a meeting of the minds.

'The Summer Fool and the Winter Fool – the King of the Road and the Queen.'

Thirteen minutes left and his only worries were the women. The man walked out of the station buffet and looked up at a clock. Providing the women didn't panic, everything was under control and he had nothing to fear.

Everything and nothing. One final blaze of glory and then the void; no more guilts, no more terrors and no more nightmares. Best of all, no more pretence, though his acting abilities had stood him in good stead. Donald Macdougal had fallen for his bait, and so had those dolts in the buffet. The man strolled on towards the lavatories. He'd met the train crew several times in the past, but they hadn't recognized him and not just on account of his beard and his dyed hair and his briefcase.

He had conned them because he was a confidence trickster. They'd believed that he was a journalist because he was playing the part of a journalist. They hadn't even asked to see his press card, and they'd accepted his hospitality willingly. A milk stout for the driver, a light ale for the co-driver, a lemonade and a cigarette for Bert Waller, the guard.

He had known what they'd drink. He'd known that Waller was a miser as well as a teetotaller. A Scrooge who'd take a cigarette from him though there were only two left in his packet. He had known that the driver was too idle to help him carry the glasses from the counter, and that his mate lacked the powers of observation. It was the man's business to know things, and he'd been completely certain that none of them would see him drop the tiny effervescent tablets into the beer, and Waller would find nothing wrong with the taste of his cigarette. The drug was virtually tasteless and its effects were rather pleasant in the early stages. The train crew would just fall quietly asleep at the proper moment and never suspect that the representative of the *Daily Globe* was responsible for their slumbers.

And why should they suspect him, or anyone else? They'd been told that a maniac had tried to reproduce an accident which had happened three years ago, but assured that the maniac was dead and there was nothing to worry about. Only the co-driver appeared slightly apprehensive and the two older men had scoffed at his quibbles.

'You're talking bleedin' nonsense, Frank. In my opinion there wasn't any loonie involved, and it was a simple case of panic, Mr ... Mr Simon.' Albert Waller pulled at his cigarette while the man repeated his name. 'I knew Bill Smith and I knew his father, and that boy worshipped his dad. They should never have put him in charge of the 9.15, because the thought of Peter's derailment was preying on his mind, and he started to imagine things. That's why Bill stopped the train, and the story of a wrecker was put out to reassure the public.

'Blimey! If passengers begin to believe our expresses are driven by neurotics, we'd soon be out of business.'

'But what about the chaps they found last night, Mr Waller?' The co-driver remained unconvinced. 'They were real enough.'

'That was murder or suicide, Frank, and if every stiff who gets killed by a train was a wrecker, there'd be fifty crashes a year. A human body can't knock a locomotive off the rails, Mr Simon, and I think the publicity department was wrong to issue its statement, because it might give other people ideas.

'Bad people, though don't quote me on that, Mr Simon. I want no trouble from the unions or the blasted Racial Discrimination Board.' In spite of his caution, Waller glared at several other occupants of the room. Two quiet Chinese girls sipping tea, three turbaned Pakistanis, and a drunken, red-faced man crooning 'Kathleen Mavourneen' to the fury of a gigantic West Indian barmaid. 'Foreigners who should have stayed in their own jungles and left us in peace. Chinks, wogs, niggers and Paddies; and the Paddies are the worst of the lot. Bloody Irishmen with bombs. Those are the bastards who scare me, and do you know why Kathleen Mavourneen's sodding fields are so fresh and green, Mr Simon?' He grinned sourly as the singer was refused another drink. 'Because her brats are all over here, trampling on ours.'

Bombs! Albert Waller was right to be scared, the man who called himself Simon thought after he'd entered a lavatory cubicle and bolted the door behind him. He rather admired the I.R.A., though he had no Irish ancestry. Not to the best of his knowledge, and that was a poor best. He knew a great deal about other people, but little about himself and didn't really want to know. There were spots in his brain which darkened when things became unbearable, and one of those things was a woman.

A woman or *two* women? He wasn't sure which woman had led him to the gates of hell and might throw him through the gates if she weakened and betrayed him. Perhaps he should have killed the women, but there was no point in brooding on that now; he had to trust them.

No point ... no time. There was a job to be done and the fingers of space and time were approaching, rushing towards him like a train. His train, though it was guarded by a dolt named Albert Waller. A dolt who would probably die because he'd accepted a cigarette and many people would die with him.

Innocent people who were not responsible for his sufferings, so why should he harm them? The man unlocked the briefcase, but he didn't release the catches immediately. There was still time to defy destiny if he had the courage, and he sat down on the lavatory bowl and prayed for courage.

'Let this cup be taken from me,' he whispered, though he knew that the request could not be granted and human voices would answer him. 'I'll flog you ... I'll break you ... I'll beat the daylights out of you unless yer do what I say' ... 'I love you, and you must kill them for my sake, darling.' 'Paddies ... Bloody Irishmen with bombs.'

No, he wasn't Irish, not to the best of his knowledge, but orders were orders. His hatred was far more bitter than any I.R.A. Provisional's and Bert Waller was a prophet as well as a fool.

'Fair enough, Belle,' he said, opening the case and smiling at the things inside it. There would be a sort of bomb on the 9.15, and the bomb was set to explode on the Crematorium Bend.

Twenty

He had crossed the hall and climbed the stairs with the gun at his back and the voice in his ears. He had walked along a dimly lit landing and halted before a door when the voice told him to. He had opened the door and seen nothing but darkness while he stood in the doorway. Then a light had been switched on and he gasped.

'All my own work, Colonel, and isn't it pretty? A memento of our last holiday.' The voice was full of pride, but Vayne's senses seemed to have failed him again. He didn't hear the words and not only his ears were faulty. There was something wrong with his eyes or his brain, because what he saw was an illusion. The strangest room he had ever entered.

The carpet was half-blue and half-yellow to give an impression of sea and sand and the ceiling above was as blue as a Mediterranean sky. There were no windows, but he felt he had stepped out on to a Spanish beach, because the walls were painted panoramas: white houses, little brown hills, and yachts sailing on the sea. The room was a stage set, but it wasn't the décor that shocked Archie Vayne.

He gasped because there were actors on the stage. A man and a woman were lolling in deck chairs and the woman had no right to be sitting down. Not when she was standing behind him.

'You've met Mr and Mrs Smith, Colonel, so aren't you going to speak to them?' He forced himself to listen to the voice and he knew that he wasn't mad. Though the two figures in the chairs looked horribly realistic, they were not alive as he'd first imagined. Wax dummies dressed in bathing costumes ... corpses that had been embalmed or preserved by the plastic coating A.C.I.D. used to protect machinery from rust. They were dead; as dead as Simon Lent and Donnie Macdougal; as dead as Sean Brady and a boy called Ray Denton.

'Please have a word with them, Colonel. It's a treat for the poor dears to receive visitors and they've been very lonely since Simon went away.' The voice pleaded with him and then became harsh and strident. 'But they deserved to be lonely. The whole family deserves to suffer and who was the worst of them? Billy and Betty who used to play games when they were kids – fathers and mothers, doctors and patients? Innocent games till they grew up and became lovers.

'Mum who brought Simon Lent here and started all the trouble? Simon himself? Vile, spying Simon who hid a cassette machine and a camera in Billy's bedroom when Betty was with him, who let Dad hear the recording and showed him that horrible picture?

'Perhaps Dad was the worst, and he paid the dearest, as you can see for yourself, Colonel.' The pistol pushed Vayne towards the male figure and he did see. The thighs and torso were mottled with scar tissue and the left arm was as thin as a child's. 'Yes, Dad paid all right. He flogged Billy with a strap and he called Betty a sluttish whore. He said he'd murder the three of us if we were still in the house when he got back from work, Simon and Billy and Betty, Colonel Vayne – his own loving children.' The harshness vanished and the voice tittered.

'Dad didn't come back from work though ... not for a long time. Someone dropped a rock on his locomotive and they took Dad to hospital. Dad was paralysed and Mum never suspected who'd crippled him.'

'Because you killed her.' Maggie Puxton's theory was correct, Vayne conceded. Peter and Dorothy Smith had been murdered by schizophrenics who'd preserved the bodies and taken on the dead personalities. 'You killed them both and guilt drove you insane.'

'You're thinking about the boy in *Psycho*, Colonel, and you're wrong as usual. We didn't murder Mum or Dad, and I'm not insane. See for yourself. Turn round and look at me.

'Turn very slowly, Archie Vayne.' The pistol drew back and when Vayne did turn he felt no surprise. The bogus Mrs Smith had removed her grey wig and her glasses and wiped the make-up from her face. A young, fair-haired girl was smiling at him.

'No, not insane, merely practical and children should care for their parents. We had to move away because of the neighbours and there were jobs to be done. Though Mum came here in a packing case with Simon, she had to sign papers and talk to solicitors and visit Dad in hospital. That wasn't difficult. Dad's sight had been affected and he couldn't see clearly.' Betty Smith's expression saddened. 'Poor old Dad. It didn't take much of an actress to deceive a half-blind man.

'But, after Dad left hospital, the pretence had to continue. People would have been suspicious if he and Mum never went out. They had to be seen in the streets and the shops and the public house, and they were. You talked to Dad in the King's Arms, Colonel, and Mum's talking to you now. Our acting was faultless and only one thing stopped the play.

'We learned our lines too well, and we never bargained for him.' Betty pointed at the space of carpet between the chairs. 'We never imagined that Simon Lent might wake up.' The pistol was also trained on the carpet and if Vayne had kept his wits he could have grabbed it from her, but he didn't. A noise made him swing round, and what he saw and heard told him that the truth was far more horrible than anything he'd believed possible.

How could a wax image open its eyes? Why was an embalmed corpse moaning?

Nearly time to go, but orders were orders and he must control his impatience and wait a little longer. The man whom the train crew knew as Mr Simon had removed his beard in the lavatory, bought a ticket to Lythborne and he stood on the platform watching passengers pass through the barrier to board the 9.15.

A larger number of passengers than he'd expected, and the *Marshal Ney* would have a fair load behind its draw-bar. Despite Albert Waller's opinion, the publicity department had done a good job. The press, radio and television had restored confidence in railway security and there had been more recent assurances that all was well with the world: a soothing female voice on the station's Tannoy and printed leaflets handed out by ticket checkers at the gates.

THE MANAGEMENT AND STAFF OF THE SOUTH-EASTERN REGION PROMISE YOU A SAFE AND COMFORTABLE JOURNEY. Mr Simon crumpled up one of the leaflets and dropped it into a litter bin, because he had a tidy nature. A place for everything and everything in its place was his favourite maxim and he left nothing to chance. The bomb would soon be in place, primed and set and ready to go off at the proper moment.

Off to sleep ... off to peace ... off to the limbo where Waller and the passengers he was supposed to guard were going. Bert Waller could have felt no ill effects yet, though the men on the locomotive must be drowsy. Liquid passed the drug into the nervous system more quickly than cigarette smoke, but Waller would be asleep

173

when the time was ripe. Bert Waller wouldn't notice *Marshal Ney* was accelerating towards the Crem Bend or suspect whose hands were on the throttle.

Not his hands of course. His left arm was paralysed and he was just a pawn. A crippled slave who had to follow instructions and plant a bomb on the 9.15.

So, whose hands would actually detonate the bomb? He considered the questions as the hand of a clock told him that the slave must start work, and he shuffled towards the locomotive dragging his maimed feet on the platform. His hands ... her hands ... their hands? Dead hands or living hands?

Yes, that was it. The man had almost reached his goal when *Marshal Ney*'s throbbing diesels gave him the answer and he nodded.

Death's hands ... Dead hands on the Dead Man's Handle ... Hands fashioned by Simon Lent.

Twenty-one

They were alive, they were breathing, and they'd been kept alive by rubber tubes forcing nourishment through their gullets. They had been washed and shaved by their daughter and they'd sat in their chairs for almost three years with a boy for company: a boy who weighed little.

Vayne believed that he knew everything now, though Peter and Dorothy Smith could not communicate – at least not to him. Doses of Solly Kahn's Terapadorm S had rotted the brain fibres and they were mere digestive systems. The man's eyes flickered, the woman moaned at times, but there was no speech and no mental activity. They were the sleeping dead, and Simon Lent had slept with them till he was lifted into another chair and wheeled to the graveyard and Donnie Macdougal's bullet. That was why Lent's body had been so light and flabby. The muscles as well as the brain were atrophied and he wouldn't have had the strength to walk a yard.

'Can't you hear them, Colonel?' Betty Smith was looking at him with genuine bewilderment. 'Don't you understand why Mum asked you to come here and what you have to do?'

'I understand that you're a murderess, my dear.' Vayne watched saliva dribble from the man's lips. 'No, worse than a murderess, Betty. You destroyed three human souls and imprisoned the bodies.'

'Wrong, Colonel. You're always wrong, but at least you're strong and that's why I want you to help me. The souls didn't die, and they're talking to us now.' She paused as though listening to a faint voice in her ear. 'Mum's pleading for a proper sleep, and Dad's shouting orders as usual. He's telling Billy to break a speed record and derail an express train.

'A train you're paid to protect, Colonel, so earn your salary and stop it. I know how strong your hands are, but you need courage, too; the courage to kill them.

'To kill them ... kill us. Strangle us ... choke us to death with your strong hands. Use any method you like, but kill Mum and Dad and release me from this hell, this misery.' Betty's voice changed and in spite of her blonde hair and smooth unwrinkled skin, Vayne knew that the mother was speaking to him through the daughter's mouth.

Possession – telepathy – schizophrenia. The causes of mania were unimportant, but the results could be disastrous, because Betty had not worked alone. Unless he could humour her and grab the pistol, there'd be another wreck on the Crematorium Bend.

'You're still talking nonsense, Colonel. How could Billy and I kill Mum and Dad, our own parents?' The girl's normal tone returned and she frowned at his question. 'Billy was angry and frightened when he dropped that rock from the bridge, and I hardly knew what I was doing when I put Terapadorm into Mum and Simon's coffee.

'No, that's not true. I took the stuff home after Mr Macdougal told me about Simon. We wanted to keep him quiet and I thought they'd all stay quiet forever.' She moved to the back of the chairs and laid a hand on her father's shoulder. 'They were quiet, too, Colonel Vayne. Quiet and peaceful till Simon ... Simple Simon Lent started to wake them up and possess us.

'The score had to be paid, but everything is so vague and blurry. I gave Billy heroin to settle Simon's account with Brady, but we couldn't kill Simon, Simon was one of the family; our own flesh and blood.

'That's why we needed Macdougal, and how he hollered when Bill hit him with the crutch and he fell towards the train. Your crutch and your train, Dad.' She whispered into the unconscious man's ear. 'The old Channel Belle that's going to die this evening unless your ghost dies first. Unless Colonel Vayne uses his big strong hands and kills you.'

'I'll kill your parents, Betty, but not with my hands.' Vayne braced himself to spring for the pistol. 'I can lay the ghosts, but I can't strangle them, and you must trust me. Give me the gun, Betty Smith.

'Good girl ... Yes, that's my good sensible lassie ... that's my pretty sweetheart.' Vayne smiled because the act was succeeding and violence should be unnecessary. The girl trusted him, and she was smiling back at him. She was holding the gun out for him and in a moment he could rush down the stairs, pick up the phone and tell Morcom or the station manager to stop the train.

Such a sensible girl ... such a pity that her face suddenly seemed to alter and grow old. What a surprise he had when a middle-aged woman raised the muzzle of the pistol and fired.

He was lying on a Spanish beach and the sand was hot, though not as hot as the sun which was scorching his flesh and searing his eyes. Blind eyes, because he was trapped in a tomb with Simon Lent and he would suffocate if he couldn't leave the beach and break out of the tomb. He was burning alive.

'Can you hear me, Colonel Vayne?' The voice mingled with the murmur of the sea and the echoes of trains roaring past the cemetery and it was a soft, gentle voice, though the words mocked him. 'I'm dying, Archie. The whole family is dead and dying, but we won't die alone, because you were too late and too clumsy.' He forced his eyelids open and reality returned. The woman at his side was a girl called Betty Smith and she had shot him twice. One bullet had entered his shoulder and the second had grazed his forehead and stunned him. But before fainting he'd fought a good fight and the pistol's six chambers were empty. The gun had been fired wildly during the struggle and the sleepers were really sleeping. Peter Smith's useless brain cells were spattered on the wall, and Betty had broken her mother's heart; literally as well as metaphorically. Blood was oozing through the chair canvas on to the blue-yellow, sea-sand carpet.

Blood was also oozing from the daughter's mouth. The last bullet had pierced her lungs and her last words were scarcely audible. 'Too late, Colonel, because we're on our way. Mum and Dad ... Billy and Bet ... Simon and Belle. The lovely Channel Belle carrying us down to Lythborne and the sea.'

The lips stopped moving, the lungs had ceased to function and the heart would never beat again. The sun was not so hot, the sand no longer burned him and the tomb was less stifling. He was in a cool, comfortable bed and he wanted to sleep.

'Earn your salary ... Use your strong hands, Archie Vayne. Put an end to our make-believe world of murder.' Taunts from the past made him pull himself up and stagger to the door. His watch was broken, his hands were weak and shaking and his legs gave way and he stumbled down the stairs. But he still had some time and some strength left.

Not much time – very little strength, but he had to earn his salary before he could sleep. Just enough time and enough strength to dial a number and save the 9.15?

Twenty-two

'I'm sorry, but I can't hear you, Colonel.' Ted Morcom had answered his car telephone and handed an extension to Emrys Evans who was sitting beside him. 'Either we've got a poor connection, or ... ' He didn't finish the sentence because the slurred tones of his superior made him suspect the worst. Vayne was drunk, disgustingly drunk. So drunk that he couldn't speak or think clearly and his gibberish was punctuated by grunts and groans and hiccups. 'Smith ... father and son ... mother and daughter ... Possession ... Dead ... Stop her ... Belle; must stopper ... '

'Are you ill, sir?' Morcom grinned because the worst could turn out to be the best, and Vayne might pay dearly for his debauch. 'A touch of the current flu virus, perhaps?'

'Ill ... bloody ill ... two bullets ... must ring off and send for ambulance.' Vayne croaked with self-pity. 'Belle first, though ... Must stop ... stop-per.'

'Ah, you're referring to the Channel Belle, sir, and there's no need to worry about that.' The car was parked on the Crematorium Bridge and Morcom glanced through the windscreen. A dozen men were patrolling the parapets and others were positioned along the cutting. Unnecessary precautions, in his opinion, because the would-be saboteur was dead and there was a body to prove it. Vayne must have been tipsy when he made his earlier call and now the brute was completely sozzled.

'The 9.15 is running late because the driver was told to go slow till he passes the curve, but the Belle should be

179

coming along soon and she'll make up time well before Lythborne.'

'You mean she's left ... left already? Yes, my watch is broken and you've got to listen, Ted; listen carefully.' Vayne struggled to make his requirements clear. 'When I ring off, contact the traffic controller and tell him to divert the train on to a side line.'

'Thank you, sir, but I'm going to ring off myself now, and I should advise you to go to bed and nurse your hangover.' Morcom replaced the instrument and turned to Evans. 'That's the end of Colonel Archibald Hector Vayne, Emrys. He's either drunk or crazy and I hope your union will demand his resignation.

'Divert an express indeed! Create more worry and inconvenience, when there's nothing to worry about and that's her now.' He watched the lights of a locomotive approaching the incline. 'Five minutes late because the crew were told to go easy, but they'll run her before long. They'll flog the old Belle all the way to Lythborne.'

Edward Morcom was partly right but mainly wrong, and the train crew were taking it easy. Albert Waller had started to feel drowsy after the guard's van slid away from the platform and the driver and his mate were unconscious before their reliefs joined them. Two men lay on the floor of the cab, three men sat at the controls, but the relief drivers did not know that they were a trinity housed in a single body.

Billy Smith certainly didn't know whose hand was on the throttle when the signal turned to green and *Marshal Ney* snorted and rumbled over the Thames towards the cemetery where Simon Lent had been hidden, towards the curve where Dad had been crippled. He'd never wanted to harm Dad, and it was all Simon's fault ... Simon's and Betty's. Simon had split on him, and Bet had persuaded him to throw that rock from the parapet. Bill and Bet, Mum and Dad and Simon. They were all to blame and damn them all ... Damn the lot of them.

Wicked Betty ... Simple Simon ... Lazy Mum and Dad dozing in their deck chairs while he was working. Stupid Billy Smith who had to obey orders as usual, though he wasn't really stupid.

He hated trains, but he knew how to drive them and he mustn't hurry till the targets were in sight. The bridge and the curve beyond the bridge, the Crem Bend. If he went too fast a passenger might panic and pull the communication cord. Dad would be angry if that happened and he'd get another flogging. He had to beat Dad's record, but bide his time.

And the time was almost ripe. There was the bridge, there was the cemetery and here were his final orders. 'Get crackin', lad,' said a voice behind him. 'Don't yer realize we're runnin' late and there's a schedule to keep?

'Nay, yer don't care about schedules, Bill. You and Simon are a brace of cowardly weaklings with no pride and no guts, but Simon's gone and Ah'm in charge. Ah'm the King and Ah'll show yer what a Warrior diesel can do. Give me the controls and Ah'll set off our bomb – the human bomb to blast 'er.'

Billy obeyed the voice. He reached in his pocket and stuck the strip of imitation scar tissue across his forehead. He put on his dark glasses, he hunched his crippled shoulder and he braced his poor, weak legs. He swung the throttle over with his sound right hand, and he laughed as the motors started to sing and the engine accelerated towards the curve. The ghost was laid at last and he thought of the happy days that Simon Lent had ruined. Just the four of them: Mum and Dad ... Billy and Bet ... such a loving family.

Postscript

The 9.15 from London to Lythborne was derailed on the Crematorium Bend while travelling at ninety-nine miles an hour. There were thirteen coaches behind the Warrior class locomotive *Marshal Ney*, and lists of the dead and injured are still incomplete.

Guard – Albert Waller. Driver and co-driver – Peter and William Smith.